— The —
Deadly
— Five —

By
Raymond Maher

Raymond Maher

2023

 FriesenPress

Suite 300 - 990 Fort St
Victoria, BC, V8V 3K2
Canada

www.friesenpress.com

Copyright © 2020 by Raymond Maher
First Edition — 2020

Editor: Eden Maher

ISBN
978-1-5255-7594-5 (Hardcover)
978-1-5255-7595-2 (Paperback)
978-1-5255-7596-9 (eBook)

Fiction, Historical

Distributed to the trade by The Ingram Book Company

INTRODUCTION

THIS STORY IS set in the 1858 Fraser River Gold Rush in British Columbia. It is a work of fiction. It reflects real places, some historical persons, and certain events of the gold rush, but in a fictitious manner.

Five gold seekers form a partnership in the Fraser River Gold Rush. Mean Mike, Nothing Brown, Seph, Old Man Magee, and Jacque come together in an epic struggle against the forces of nature in a dangerous river and mountainous wilderness. They must travel and search the treacherous Fraser River, with its source in the isolated inland Rocky Mountain ranges of British Columbia. The Fraser rips and pushes its way from lofty mountain peaks to Hells Gate in its own canyon, and beyond to the Pacific Ocean through the Fraser Valley. A conscienceless river that shows the promise of hidden gold in its gravel bars and death for the foolhardy.

The five must face the challenge of relentless numbers of fellow gold seekers intent on getting the gold before them, and the gold found by the five. The onslaught of endless gold hunters forces the natives to defend themselves against the gold seekers invading their lands. All gold seekers struggle for daily bread, with scarce, highly priced food and supplies at the Hudson's Bay trading forts and sprouting gold rush towns beside them.

Each of the Deadly Five must face themselves, who they are as individuals, and why they are searching for gold. Each person is tested to their core when they find gold. Readers will decide if they are guilty of murder as the Deadly Five.

CHAPTER I
Delirious

"SOMEBODY IS GOING to get stinking rich, and that somebody is me!" I often say it because why shouldn't it be me getting the gold that is being found in Canada. All I want there is enough gold for a lifetime or two. I'll gamble my life in the wilderness ahead; for gold, that is all mine. Right now, I've nothing to do but to think on this here packed steamer.

Gold strikes start a race that too many are wanting to run. Many on this here ship heading for Victoria have already rushed to California for gold, but that race is over. We're in a new horse race now because we all want to grab the gold up north. I know that gold can offer me everything and anything I could ever want if I get enough of it. Some warned me that I've got "Gold Fever" or a bad case of greediness, which is blinding me to the deadly price I could pay for hunting gold in the wilderness. A few other stupid people tell me that being rich is no guarantee of happiness. I argue with them that being poor is no joy either. Some people have rocks in their heads, instead of brains, and should just shut the hell up!

It's 1859 and a good year for me to get rich. As an American, I know little about Canada. It is north of us and under British rule. It is said to be sparsely settled and mostly unexplored. Gold was found on a river there called the Fraser, and the gold strike is continuing northward along that river. It's all I need to know until I get there and find out more for myself.

Mean Mike is what I am called by those who know me. It's a name that my brothers gave me. As the oldest of thirteen children, and always big for my age, I bullied and threatened my younger brothers. I was the boss at school and more than ready to fight there to prove it. At fifteen, I was the size of a grown, tall man. Even then, no one doubted that I had both the size and strength to take care of myself.

Leaving home at fifteen was mutual good riddance between myself and my family. My family is poor and ordinary with way too many hungry mouths to feed. The only one who ever seemed to understand the slightest bit of me is my old man. He's a big, burly, Scottish blacksmith, respected for his reliable work and honest dealings at his shop. He's a hard, steady worker but loves his whiskey and fist-fighting when drunk.

From a little kid, I was called to work under my father's critical eye in his blacksmith shop. I was to work as an adult, and everything had to be done right. The old man would not accept any work that he called half-assed. Faultless workmanship was the only thing he recognized. I blamed him for making my life a miserable hell, in his hot and suffocating blacksmith shop, which was always full of his endless work and orders for me.

When I said that I was leaving home, my old man called me a stubborn, rebellious lad. He blamed it on my Scottish nature. He respected my plan to strike out on my own. He felt that he had tried to teach me blacksmithing, a good and honorable trade worthy of any man's livelihood, but I rebelled and wanted something better. To him, it was reckless, but he had been a reckless boy and young man himself. He understood not always holding the line given a person.

From the age of eight until ten when his family left for America, my father had climbed the remains of the thousand-year-old Dunbar Castle in his Scottish hometown. The kids were forbidden to climb the remaining castle's fifty-foot-high stone walls, because a child had fallen and died as a result of climbing them. That fact only made imps like my dad want to climb the ruins even more. He said that if the number had been ten deaths, that would have made climbing the walls even more exciting. It's the Scottish way to be daring, even reckless, facing the threat of danger and death.

My old man said often that it's Jesus's way to be gentle and humble in heart, but Scottish men are fighters and the equal of all men in battle and life. In war, they fight bare-assed in kilts and drink their whiskey in victory or defeat. The old man was convinced that as I set out on my own, that I could at least fight and give as good as I get or better.

I found leaving home much harder than I imagined and not nearly as satisfying as I dreamed. I quickly learned that there was truth in what my father often said about me, that I have little heart for sustained hard work. Before I left home, I was sure that it was not the hard work that I rebelled at, but that other jobs would be easier and much more interesting than blacksmithing.

The first person to give me a job when I started on my own was Mr. Lyons at his general store. He liked my size and apparent strength, eyeing me up as a good beast of burden for handling the heavy work of moving crates, boxes, cases, barrels, bags, and all other endless merchandise that his store offered to buyers. My pay was wee, but my job at the general store gave me one meal a day and a cot in the storeroom to sleep on at night.

After about three days, I was stunned at the amount of heavy lifting at the general store, and the hard work there seemed to equal the blacksmith shop. Mr. Lyons is a short square bald man with a razor-sharp tongue. He was no better to work for than my old man.

He was not afraid of my size or strength. I was to do my work or get fired. No one was going to pay me unless I worked hard. It was an ugly fact to face.

Being out on my own left me with no younger brothers to boss around and only myself to torment. My appetite for fighting found an outlet in a regular supply of fellas who came to town to raise a little hell away from their humdrum ranches and farms.

I was the big lad from the general store who liked to fight. If you want to fight, someone will take you on. The alley behind the general store was a gathering place where those who considered themselves tough and able could challenge me. I was sure that I was tough enough to hold my own with anyone in a fight. I was a danger to myself at that time and it took a bit of time for me to know it.

On this here steamer heading for Victoria, I've little to do but think and consider who I am and where I'm going. At eighteen, I've been in enough fights to know that I no longer need to prove that I can fight well. I only need to fight when it is necessary and that I need to fight sober. I am a mean drunk who stupidly picks fights that I often lose. Being drunk makes me slow-reacting and clumsy as I stumble around suffering punches I don't see coming.

I find it strange that since I left home, I find myself in demand for the blacksmithing my old man forced on me. I have the skill to shoe horses, fix broken wagon wheels or axels, and I ended up being asked to do them. I worked as a ranch hand, where I was called on to do the blacksmithing at the ranch. It was the same when I drove a stagecoach route.

I learned to keep ledgers and do inventory at the general store. Many have little ability to count and keep track of everything. At a store, you must count both what comes in and what goes out. Few folks have business sense and have no idea when to sell and when to buy. These skills, like my blacksmithing ones, bother me, for there is a part of me that rejects honest, needful work. Anyone can be a blacksmith or a store owner. I want to do what isn't ordinary. I liked searching for gold in California, the promise of getting rich through doing what was daring and dangerous.

CHAPTER 2
Crumbling Delusions

TOMORROW THE BOAT is to land in Victoria, and everyone on this overcrowded bucket is anxious to begin our hunt for gold. I've always had a tall attitude of myself. On this here ship, I feel that I can bare-knuckle fight with anyone if I need to. Few men on board are as tall or big as me. I have a steady hand with my revolver and a keen eye for any target with my rifle. I can knife fight in a pinch, but I'm better with my fists. I think that most people I meet can't even drink as much as me.

There's one man on ship equal to my size, a tormentor and a bully to others during the passage, but not to me. There is a feeling of tension as the steamer draws nearer to Victoria. It is like we are all waiting for the signal to start the race for the gold, and no one wants to be left behind.

I am staring out at the water from the rail of the upper deck this evening, thinking that this voyage feels endless.

I hear, "Move over and let someone else get the fresh air."

It is loud enough for the whole deck to hear, and a sudden quiet comes upon everyone. The one who has been a tormentor says again to a man who he is trying to bully, "Move over and let me have some air, or I'll throw you overboard."

I am watching the big guy, not paying much attention to the smaller man who is to be his victim. I gasp with everyone else as a knife flashes from the victim and is embedded in the tormentor's throat.

"What is going on there?" a sailor's voice calls as he appears on the far side of the deck.

"Not a thing!" the victim says as he shoves the big man clutching at his throat over the rail of the ship.

The victim yells across the deck to the sailor, "Come over and have a look if you want, I just dropped a piece of junk overboard."

I watch the sailor come over and look down at the water. The big guy has disappeared below the water's surface, and the sailor is satisfied and leaves. I am shocked to see the victim looking at me.

He says to me, "Bullies have a short life. You look like one to me." Then he is gone.

The Mean Mike sense of myself is turning upside down in my mind. I am suddenly not so sure of myself, and I feel I need a drink, so I set about drowning my doubts with a flask of whiskey that I always carry with me. There is a small part of the deck that is avoided because seawater can spray over that area, showering those who are there. For the moment, it is dry and only one small man is sitting on the floor, his back against the side of the deck, reading a letter. I sit down, making sure to keep a good space from him. He looks up from the letter he is reading and nods. I nod in return and take a swig from my whiskey flask.

I put the flask away in my pocket and say, "My mother never taught me to share. My family calls me Mean Mike, and mean is how I like myself."

"I don't drink anything stronger than coffee, which can be as bitter as death when you're half asleep and trying to wake up on a cattle drive. My family calls me Will, but because of my small size, mostly I'm called Nothing Brown. I'm never getting any bigger, but there will always be some dumb cuss to call me, Nothing Brown. The name has followed me from the goldfields in California."

"Did ya strike it rich there?" I ask.

"I made a little money there, barely enough to enable me to try again now for more gold in Canada. It seems like you might have been in California trying to get rich yourself," questions Nothing Brown.

"I got some gold there. Just enough to know that hunting gold is for me," I say as I take several swallows of whiskey. "What do ya know about the gold strike ahead of us?" I ask him.

"I have been reading a letter from my friend Frank who has been there since the end of April. He says the Fraser River is dangerous. When it is at its full height, no canoe or boat can get up or down it. When the river is at low levels, it has gravel and sandbars where the gold is found. My friend said for me to come in the summer when the water is lower."

"How far into the interior of the country do gold hunters need to go?" I ask.

"My friend says from the mouth of the Fraser River to Fort Langley is thirty miles; from there to Fort Hope is sixty miles; from Fort Hope to Fort Yale is a day's travel; from there to the forks where the Fraser River meets the Thompson River, eight day's travel. From Fort Yale to the forks, the Fraser River has dangerous rapids where many have died. The search for gold goes farther north but with more opposition from the Indians and the difficulty of dangerous mountain trails."

"Ain't there any roads into the gold country?" I ask.

"The further you go inland, there are no roads," Nothing Brown answers.

My mind is now going a bit fuzzy from the thirsty drinking of my whiskey, and I'm now feeling mean towards Nothing Brown. I decide he knows way more than me about what is to come in the search for gold, and I tell him abruptly to shut up for I have heard all I want. He says nothing more and gets up to leave. I stagger to my feet and grab him by the front of his shirt and hold him up in the air off the floor. His nickname is right, as there is no weight to him at all. I set his feet back down on the floor, let go of his shirt, and start to say, "I could've thrown you overboar—"

I do not get "overboard" all the way out of my mouth because Nothing Brown slugs me with the force of a horse-kick in my nuts. I double over, feeling like my nuts are busted open, yet I realize with my head lowered down, Nothing Brown has punched me in my nose and blood is flowing freely from it. Adding to my injury, Nothing Brown brings his knee up under my chin, bouncing my head back so that it hits the wall. I fall to my knees and think I will stay put awhile.

Nothing Brown says to me, "Stay sober if you want to bully people, Mike, or you'll get your nuts kicked." I think he's right, and I will avoid this Nothing Brown in the future if I'm tipsy. I might not be mean enough to handle him.

CHAPTER 3
One Among Many

THEY SAY THAT gold is for the taking ahead of us, but first, we must get to Victoria, for the search begins from there. This boat is said to be carrying over 1700 gold seekers. I know one who will be off to a slow start once this boat docks at Victoria tomorrow. Lying beside me is Mean Mike, fitfully sleeping in his drunkenness, suffering from a bruised nose, head, and testicles. I contributed to his bruising even though they call me Nothing Brown. Sadly, I'm the one who is seeking to become a light of love and peace in my dealings with others.

I feel Mean Mike is my responsibility, as passed out drunks are often the target of thieves on such a packed ship as this. Every character here, traveling to the goldfields, is unique, but some have nothing more than the clothes on their backs. As a Quaker, I believe in simplicity and humility, but too many come with nothing, expecting to steal their daily bread from others. I must clarify that I'm a Quaker under discipline. I have had a problem with self-control and restraint in my life. I have no problem ignoring card-playing, dancing, and liquor. I'm industrious, thrifty, and honest, but I have a trigger-happy temper that explodes and results in violent actions towards others.

I had to leave the fellowship of the Friends or the Society of Friends as others call us Quakers in Oregon. There are only a few of us in Oregon, but more will continue to settle there. We are people of extended family and kinship. Quaker brothers have successfully brought fruit trees to the Pacific coast, and my family and a few others are gathered there as kin and kind of them.

I need to set an example in my family, and in the meetings and fellowship of our faith, by living in the light of Christ in my actions. Where is my spiritual growth in pacifism and seeing God in everyone? It is a struggle I have yet to win. I seek gold, not for myself, but that I can give it away in charity. My elders feel if I can obtain gold and yet remain humble and simply give it for the blessing of others, I will reach more maturity in a faithful life. They believe I must learn to act as if any violence on my part is unjustifiable under any circumstance. I must settle all disputes with others by peaceful means. I must gain a peaceful heart by acting strife-free in the grabbing and pushing for gold in the days ahead.

Yes, I will be challenged to act with self-control among a stampede of hungry gold seekers. I will pray and meditate with my Bible until morning. I confess that I failed in dealing nonviolently with Mean Mike earlier this evening. I must begin to live in Christ's light of grace with others. There are no more excuses for me! I must pray for an outpouring of the Holy Spirit to empower me. May God help me to stop responding with an eye for an eye and a tooth for a tooth when dealing with others.

"Excuse me, may I have a word with you?" I hear and see a man of middle age addressing me.

He continues, "I believe I know of you from the Willamette Valley in the Oregon country. I'm from the French Prairie near the Willamette River. My family is one of a number from fur traders, trappers, and company employees who were with the Hudson's Bay Company at the Willamette fur post that closed in 1833. We farm the land around where the post once stood. Our way of life in the fur trade is vanishing. Your numbers as Quakers are small in the valley, but you show respect to the natives and breeds like me. You do not sell whiskey to the Indians or seek to cheat them of their land. It is Quakers who brought fruit trees to plant, which is most amazing and welcome. More and more settlers rush into the valley like grasshoppers gobbling up everything in their path as if only they count. Sorry, I have spoken too much about myself and the valley, but I wondered if you have any partners for the gold search ahead?"

"I have been thinking about that myself," I answer. "My friend who is prospecting farther north on the Fraser since April sent me word in a letter that provisions are expensive inland, and every party of miners should start with supplies to last three or four months. We should travel in the largest sized canoes as the small ones are liable to swamp in rapids. Each canoe should have about 150 to 200 feet of strong line for towing over swift water. There have been difficulties with Indians both attacking the miners and stealing their supplies, so he cautions me that all must be well armed. It is my understanding we need five or six men to row the treacherous Fraser River to reach Fort Hope and on to Fort Yale. My friend says that they keep finding gold beyond Fort Yale, and it seems to be where all the excitement is building. It is time to look for partners, for I do not have other partners that I am traveling with either. The sleeping drunk beside me calls himself Mean Mike. I think he might join us as he is less mean lately. I would be glad to work with you at Victoria and gather others as partners for our trip inland," I state.

"My name is Jacque, and I have a tent and a few other supplies like pemmican with me. Me and canoes go together like bees and honey as I was nearly born in one. I hope to find a little gold, but I go to travel the wilderness. I seek the wilds as they are the sacred places that God alone knows. Once people invade the wilderness, they end up destroying it. Thank you for our talk. We will meet tomorrow after docking."

I say, "Good night," and turn my mind back to meditation and prayer.

CHAPTER 4
A Tent City

"I FIND IT hard to believe we are at a city of tents," I say, standing on the shore at Victoria at last. Beside me are Jacque and Mean Mike, who are also surprised at the sheer number of gold seekers camped out here waiting to be registered and obtain a license to hunt for gold before they go further. It becomes apparent as we ask those about us that we are to be aware we are on Canadian soil and under the authority of the British colonies. Jacque has been here at Fort Victoria years ago when it was called Fort Albert, and, also once since it was called Fort Victoria. Jacque still knows a few of the Hudson's Bay employees. They have told him that last year on April 25, the first of the gold seekers arrived as the townspeople were returning home from church. That day a ship docked at Victoria's harbor. Four hundred and fifty men, about equal to the population of the settlement, disembarked with backpacks containing blankets, miners' pans, spades, and firearms. They began an influx of gold seekers that has grown into the thousands since then. Last year gold seekers searched the lower reaches of the Fraser River from New Westminster to Fort Hope and beyond to Fort Yale. Now the search goes further north of Fort Yale.

The three of us agree that with a canoe, we can make our way up the Fraser River to Fort Yale. We can keep an eye peeled for gold that might have been missed by those who have gone before us. Water levels in the river can hide gravel bars or ridges that contain gold. We suspect that we will need to get beyond Fort Yale to find gold in earnest. We could take a steamer from Victoria to New Westminster at the mouth of the Fraser River. It is dangerous to cross there by canoe, but Jacque has done it before. He admits it can be difficult, but he is up for it. Mean Mike and I are willing to try it with him. We will need at least two others to join us in our travel by canoe.

Jacque will secure the canoe. Mean Mike will scout out where we can get the best price on supplies. He feels that his store experience can help us in obtaining supplies. I think I have the patience to wait in line to secure our licenses. Mean Mike stood in line yesterday and got into a shoving match and two fistfights. I am prepared to stay in line during the day and overnight. Mike and Jacque must take turns spelling me off as we inch our way to the license issuer.

Jacque's tent is large enough to sleep the three of us, and we hope to set out by canoe in a few days, for life in Victoria is like being in a beehive with endless bees all swarming back and forth. Nothing matters but getting set to fly away for gold. After four days, Mean Mike has met a fellow named Ed, who is back at Victoria with gold for the assayer's office here. He is eager to return up the Fraser and is open to join us in our travel by canoe. I have talked with a man in the lineup for our licenses named Seph, a bartender. He is sick of serving drinks and enforcing the removal of those that want to ruin the bar for countless reasons. He is a large, tough man in the cut of a large size like Mean Mike.

It is now seven days of staying here at Victoria, and we are ready to set off from here by canoe. I have little experience with rowing a boat. Jacque and Ed are experienced. Mean Mike and Seph claim to be experienced, but as we paddle away from land and get surrounded by endless water in every direction, I notice they are both sweating and looking green. I have more than enough trouble rowing and keeping up with the others. There is little talk in the canoe because three of us are terrified and ready to throw up. Ed and Jacque just act like rowing this canoe is as natural as walking. They are so comfortable one would think that they could walk on water should the canoe sink. My mind is fixed on scripture, and Jesus saying, "Fear Not."

Then Jacque says, "Well, voyagers, you're doing good, but the real test of canoeing is getting back in your boat after she tips over."

Ed pipes up, "When I went up the Fraser in a canoe the first time the damn currents and the high river tipped our canoe six times. Even being dunked in the cold river six times did nothing for the smell of Old Man Magee in our canoe. He smelled worse after each spill into the river. Funny thing though, when we capsized the seventh time, we couldn't reach him, and we were sure he was done for, but the fish threw him back in our canoe. I think they were sturgeons which come as big as whales in the Fraser."

Seph asks earnestly, "What'll we do if the canoe should capsize?"

"Just close your mouth, so you don't choke on water. Open your eyes and kick your feet and swing your arms. It is called swimming, and swim to the canoe," Jacque replied.

"What if I don't swim to the canoe?" asks Mean Mike.

"Then swim for the shore, and if you cannot see the shore, just keep swimming, and the canoe will find you. Somebody out of the five of us will reach the canoe and come after you," Ed answers.

"How many reached your seven overturned canoes besides Old Man Magee?" I ask.

"Well, you can see I did, and most of the others did most of the time. We lost two men to the river, and Old Man Magee was not one of them," Ed answers.

The talk ends abruptly, as Mean Mike throws up over the side of the canoe and loses his oar in the process. We turn the boat around and retrieve his paddle, which was floating on the water.

We had no idea that Jacque was looking out for us inexperienced canoe travelers. He knew there are six large islands in the Georgia Strait between Victoria and the mainland of British Columbia. He was directing us to two of the islands on our way across the strait. The first island we came to after hours of rowing was the south end of a large island divided in two with an isthmus. It was the home of the natives or Salish people who had traded with Jacque as an agent of the Hudson's Bay Company. He spoke with them, and they gave us fish to eat at our camp at the southern tip of the island. Three of us were beat with blistered hands, aching arms, and convinced that we must present an image that there was nothing hard about traveling by canoe. Jacque and Ed lingered around the fire after supper, me, Seph, and Mean Mike were asleep like dead men. We awake to a thunderstorm with heavy rain and strong winds this morning. It is early afternoon as we push off from the island.

This, our second day of canoeing, is harder than our first because the water is rougher, and more water has come into the boat with the high waves. Today, I am to bail out the water that invades the canoe. I am continually busy with this impossible task. It seems that the more water I bail out of the boat, the more it comes in to frustrate me. It is at sunset that we reach a second island. It is called by the natives Long Nose Island and is the island closest to the mainland. Jacque says it is about fifty miles of empty water to the mainland from here. When we reach the coast, then we will travel north to the mouth of the Fraser at New Westminster. With good luck, it will take around twelve hours to reach the mainland. Jacque wants to know if we need a day of rest before the hardest part of the trip, but we are divided on what to do. Ed is opposed to any delay. Jacque says it is our choice because he is game if we are, but that we may need to row hard at times, and our lives will depend on our strength and endurance. He would rather wait a day than have our strength play out on us when we need it most.

I say that I favor a day of rest but will go along with what the majority wants. Seph seconds my statement that he could use a day of rest. Mean Mike sides with Ed saying that he wants to go on without the day's delay. We have two in favor of resting and two in favor of pushing onwards come morning. Jacque said since he is neutral, we could flip a coin. Everyone seemed okay with that until those in favor or a day of rest won the flip. Ed turned both angry and nasty, saying that he has sure as hell joined up with a bunch of gutless gold hunters needing a day of rest. He promises that when we have reached New Westminster, he will be parting company with us.

Jacque is neither surprised nor offended. He says that we have thrown in together, but there is nothing to stop anyone from leaving if they want. He offers that if Ed wants to leave us before New Westminster that he is welcome to go. Ed mutters that New Westminster will suit him fine.

CHAPTER 5
Morning Visitors

OUR DAY OF rest is no day of rest. We awake to the sound of shouting from a canoe on the water just offshore. The men in the boat are asking if they can come ashore at our camp. Jacque and Ed are up, and the rest of us get up quickly. Jacque cautions us to have our guns handy. "Be careful of visitors," he whispers to us. Ed calls for them to come ashore.

Three men land their canoe and come into our camp. Two of the three have full black beards. The other man has a large handlebar mustache. They are dressed in buckskin and wear moccasins on their feet. They ask if we might have coffee to share. They claim that they spent the night on the water and are lost trying to canoe across to the mainland.

Jacque, having spent years in the Hudson's Bay Company, has already made strong black tea for us. He offers the visitors tea, and they accept it. One of the men has been doing all the talking for the three of them. I wonder if he is the oldest or the boss of them in some way.

He asks, "Would any of you men be open to guiding us to the mainland for pay?" None in our group offers to guide them.

Jacque says, "We plan to leave tomorrow morning for the mainland, and you can follow our canoe if you want."

The spokesman of the three says, "Thanks for the offer to follow you. We'll talk it over between us as we drink our tea and take a quick rest." The men give the impression of being quiet and honorable. They share that they too are heading for the Fraser and the gold rush. Soon their tea is finished, and they rise from our campfire, thank us for the tea. It seems they are leaving us, and I think that I'm so ready for this day of rest ahead.

Before I finish my thoughts of resting, our visitors transform themselves from quiet guests with tin cups in their hands to pistol-holding thieves. We are caught completely off guard.

"We want your canoe because ours leaks, and we'll take your supplies and money. Hand over your guns and knives to the boys here beside me now," their spokesman orders us.

I knew it was time for me to take a fit. I have spent a lifetime of perfecting my performance of taking a fit. I shriek loud enough to startle the dead. I flail and convulse myself, flop, and flap on the ground, and fling myself in circles. I mimic a chicken with its head chopped off.

Mean Mike is quick to help with my diversion to distract the thieves. He yells, "Look out! Nothing is taking another fit, watch, he bites like a dog!"

It is enough to distract the men with their pistols, and Ed, Jacque, and Seph rush at them and wrestle with them.

Mike rushes into the struggle to disarm the robbers, but he trips and falls into Ed and Jacque, knocking the gun out of the hand of one of the robbers by hitting the pistol with his head. As Mike falls from his stumble, he knocks Ed and Jacque down to the ground by landing on top of them. Thus, he frees the man with the mustache that Ed and Jacque have been fighting.

I begin barking like a dog and start to run at the mustached man who has lost his pistol, and he seems to think I am the devil himself and will bite him. He takes off for the woods and disappears out of sight.

While Ed and Jacque are yelling at Mean Mike to get the hell off them, Seph proves his talent as a previous saloon bartender. He successfully knocks the heads of the two bearded men together, putting them in an out-cold sleep.

It turns out Mean Mike hit his head not only on the gun but on the ground when he tripped and went down. Seph and I roll him off Ed and Jacque, who claim Mike weighs as much as a horse, and that they almost suffocated under his weight. A little water revives Mean Mike, and he has a huge goose egg on his forehead.

Ed looks at the two thieves out cold and announces, "I'm going to shoot these two and the other one if he shows his face."

"No, don't," I say, "there's no need to shoot or harm them more! Let's just start for the mainland and leave them here."

"They don't deserve to be left to live," Ed insists, "I'll kill them! Let it be on me."

"I agree with Nothing Brown," Jacque speaks up, "no need for bloodshed. We can skip the day of rest and leave these guys here."

Seph agrees saying, "Leave them here, and let's just go."

We can see once again that Ed is angry at us but holds his tongue and starts packing up camp with us and loading the canoe. As we begin paddling toward the mainland, we are blessed with quiet, calm water. Seph breaks the silence in the canoe by recounting various fights he has been entangled in as a bartender. He believes that drinking men either turn happy and generous or mean and belligerent. He also found that few quit drinking before they are drunk and are not fully aware of what they are doing. Many can never remember what they said or did when they were drunk. The next day, they say that their words and fists weren't personal; they were just drunk.

Mean Mike tells us how his dad drinks, then tries to fistfight with everyone and anyone to prove how good he is at fighting. He wins often and loses just as often, but never gets tired of fighting when he is drunk. Seph agrees that alcohol does that to about half the drinkers. Mean Mike confesses that he turns mean when he drinks. When he takes a drink or two of liquor, he becomes desperate for more like a man dying of thirst.

Jacque says that he will have some drinks with his friends but holds liquor as a great evil spirit. He has seen the destruction the firewater has brought to Indian tribes and in his own family. He has also seen the fights fur trappers have had because they were drunk and ended up destroying their partnerships, leaving wounds, and even killing one another.

Ed has been silent and seems to be brooding over the fact that he did not have a chance to shoot the thieves. When asked if he has anything to share, Ed lets lose with biting words. He announces, "I have no respect for the fools who waste their money on drink. Old Man Magee that I spoke of as stinking so bad that seven dunks in the river couldn't make him smell any better, smelled of sour whiskey and urine. He, like the rest of us, found gold on the Fraser but wasted it on drink. A few drinks and Old Man Magee could not stop drinking until his money vanished. When I saw him last, he was at Fort Yale dead broke and hungry. He was begging for a handout, and I said to him, 'Starve, you old drunk.'"

Mean Mike asked, "What'd he say to ya?"

He said, "I helped you reach the canoe when it overturned the last time in the river. I was an old drunk then too, you prick!"

"So, you didn't help him?" I asked

"I don't help drunks, nor spare the lives of worthless thieves! I believe the only good Indian is a dead one, and I only tolerate breeds if it fits my purpose. I'm using the gold I find to invest in sluice boxes and the equipment to mine the deeper gold below the surface. I'm not here to get a little rich and be gone. I plan to be here until all the deeper, purer gold is mine. I will travel and partner with like-minded men after New Westminster, not with you four spineless jokers."

Jacque amazes me when he says, "Thanks for letting us know where we stand with you. I like your honesty. I'd rather know open dislike than a false friend. Seems to me Old Man Magee has you pegged rightly, but until we reach the Fraser, we need to work together." Then Jacque changes the subject like he is as smooth as a diplomat and says to me, "Nothing Brown, tell us how you come to be such a convincing fit-taker."

So, I explain, "That's thanks to being short and a Quaker. Short kids get no respect, especially if they are brought up to keep from cursing and taking God's name in vain. Boys are wise about watching their tongues before adults, but when no adults are around, a boy is expected to curse with the best of them. My small size was against me, and my lack of bad language was unnatural to other kids. Our Quaker ways of speaking up against slavery, honoring women as equal partners in marriage, wanting fair treatment of natives made me and my family disagreeable to a considerable number of people."

The men are listening to me, so I continue, "There were always some who wanted to fight me or knock my stupid ideas right out of me. I hated being picked on so, one day, when a bigger kid was about to beat me up, I snapped. I screamed so loud that I could not be ignored. The bully knew with my shrieking and wailing the teacher would come, and any other adults who happened to be near. He went to put his hand over my mouth, and I bit his hand, and he was stunned because I had never defended myself before.

"I threw myself on the ground, flailing and convulsing and pretending to act like a chicken with its head chopped off. My attacker backed up, and the other kids all yelled, 'Will Brown has gone crazy! He is taking a fit!'

"That is the way the teacher found us, and she watched in horror, not knowing what to do with me. So, I stopped suddenly jumped up in the air, then went stiff and straight and started howling like a wolf and staring at the boy who was holding his bitten hand.

"He started yelling, 'Don't let him bite me again; maybe he has rabies.' All the other kids ran for the protection of the schoolhouse, and the teacher fainted. I knew right then and there; people will leave you alone if they know you could throw a fit or go crazy in their sight. Rabies works too, but I wouldn't recommend it."

The men are now laughing, and I tell them, "Mean Mike saw me throw a fit once at Victoria, while I was waiting in line to get us registered and to get our licenses to search for gold. Mike had a pushing match and two fistfights while waiting in line. When I took over for him, a few people thought they could push me out of line, so I had to throw a fit. I gave my best performance because I wanted people in sight of me to know I could go crazy and start a fuss. Mean Mike loved my performance and asked if I threw another one when he was near if he could yell, 'Look out if he foams at the mouth, he'll start biting.'

"Today those thieves were so slick, it looked like they would take all we had, maybe even our lives, so I threw a fit. I'm just glad you guys used it to our advantage. As a Quaker, I'm to settle all disputes peacefully without any violence. I have a temper that can flare up and out of control, and I do resort to violence sometimes. I'm not proud that I lose control of my anger. It is my shame."

"He's not kidding about having a lightning temper. Watch out because he specializes in busting nuts," Mean Mike said with all sincerity.

CHAPTER 6
Canoe Trip

OUR EASY CANOEING lasts for a long spell, but then Jacque predicts that we are about halfway to the mainland. Around that point, the wind begins to pick up, and the water goes from calm to unsettled. The waves start rolling, and our canoe is bouncing off them as if they have every intention of blocking us from ever seeing the mainland. The rowing is hard and heavy to keep us going in the right direction, and I'm bailing water from the canoe to keep us afloat. Time seems to stand still, and it is a strain and struggle to exhaustion. We are held like a leaf on the ocean, rowing furiously in our canoe and going nowhere.

"There's a storm coming for us," Jacque yells, and we all become aware of a new reality approaching. The sky darkens. Sheets of rain come towards us, and none of us says a word while we cling to life in our open canoe. The rain stings and drenches us.

Mean Mike yells, "Say a prayer, Nothing, every time you bail out water."

"For you or me?" I yell back.

"For all of us!" he answers.

"You can pray as well as me," I holler into the wind and rain.

"No need for everybody to bother God," he calls.

"I'll do it, but don't complain to me if you don't like His answer," I yell.

I have been silently praying for a safe trip to the coastland. The fact that there is a devil of a storm upon us tests my willingness to trust God when things go from bad to worse. I keep praying that God will be merciful to us as the storm rages around us, and I keep bailing water out of the canoe.

I'm not sure if it has been hours or days, but I hear Jacque yell, "Rest, for the storm is almost done, and you'll have lots more rowing ahead." He is right; the sky has lightened, and the water is less turbulent, the wind has died down, and I'm thankful. All of us are tired and soaking wet and not quite sure how much more we can give.

"Another hour or two, and we will make the mainland," Jacque tells us. It sounds good to me; it gives me hope we can make it.

Mean Mike announces his head is hurting him, and he is feeling sick. He passes out from pain and exhaustion, slumping to one side of the canoe, which begins to tip it. Jacque wants to keep Mean Mike's deadweight from overturning the boat, so he jumps into the water and swims beside the canoe where Mike is slumped over.

The rest of us keep paddling, trying to keep the canoe heading for the mainland, while Jacque is in the water fighting to keep the canoe upright.

After some time, Jacque calls for us to stop, as he is tired out from swimming and holding up the canoe. He says, "Throw some water on Mean Mike and see if we can revive him enough to have him sit up straight." The bailing bucket is passed to Ed, who is closest in the canoe to Mean Mike. Ed scoops water from the ocean into the bucket and throws the water at Mike.

Mean Mike awakes with such a start that he jumps up and the canoe tips. We all go into the ocean with Jacque. Ed and Jacque swim well, while Seph and I tread water, and Mean Mike splashes and thrashes about yelling, "What the hell hit me?"

Jacque is quick to right the canoe. He orders me to climb in, which I do. Next, Jacque tells Ed to join me in the boat. He and Seph get Mean Mike quieted down and help him into the boat. Seph gets in and Jacque is the last. We have lost some of our paddles and supplies to the ocean. Thankfully, we're all alive, and we take turns with the oars that we have left to row for the mainland.

I see the moon is up as Jacque says to us, "That dark stretch ahead is the coastline of British Columbia. We are almost there."

We are not able to find a place to land along the shore for a long time. At last, we pull the canoe up on a beach and stagger along the solid ground. We are too exhausted to set up our camp, so we drop and fall asleep on the sand.

I dream of home and family, and warmth, and food, and belonging, and sharing. I awake to an overcast morning with a cool breeze blowing on us off the water. Mean Mike still has a goose egg on his forehead and looks ill. Jacque and Seph have wrapped a blanket around him and are ready to give out our strong black tea to start the day. Our food supply bundle was lost in the ocean when the canoe tipped. The only food left is what's left of Jacque's pemmican. The food bundle is a costly loss for it was to last us for two or three months.

Ed wants to get started for the Fraser and New Westminster right away, and Seph and Jacque want to let Mean Mike rest for a couple of hours before we start in the canoe again. Ed asks Mean Mike, "Can you sit up and not tip the canoe if we start now?"

Mean Mike answers, "Yeah!"

It takes us the whole day to reach New Westminster. When we arrive, Ed quickly leaves us, like we have both lice and leprosy that he could catch from us. Seph stays with the canoe, as there are so many people here. Everyone in New Westminster seems to be ready to go up the Fraser or have come down it. There are men here for the assayer's office with their gold panned from the Fraser.

Jacque and I take Mean Mike to a doctor, for he has double vision and a pounding headache. The bump on his head is still prominent. The doctor we find is both expensive and busy. He wants five dollars before he will look at Mean Mike. We pay up, and he checks Mike out and announces he has a concussion. He says Mike needs to lie quiet and still for maybe a week to let the swelling in his brain disappear. He will tell us after a week if he will be okay.

Jacque, me, and Mean Mike had gone together to buy our canoe, and we have also paid equal parts collectively for a food bundle to keeps us going on our gold search. Ed and Seph joined us to help with the rowing cross from Victoria to the Fraser River and up the Fraser. Ed did not want to stick with us after New Westminster and Seph might leave us as we need to delay, giving Mean Mike a chance to get better. Seph hears what the doctor said and is willing to wait with us until Mike is ready to travel again. Seph wants not only to go on with us but to partner with us. We are pleased.

Finding a spot to set up our tent and place our canoe beside it at New Westminster takes us the rest of the day. We also need a cot or mattress for Mike to rest on to get better. Seph thinks that he might be able to get a bed for Mike. He sets off for a tour of the many saloons in New Westminster and returns later with an old rope cot that we fear might break under Mean Mike's weight and size.

Seph is sure that the cot will be strong enough, for it is used at one of the saloons for prostitution. It has survived double weight and bouncing in the past. Seph was able to borrow it for a week while the saloon is short of a prostitute. He also landed a job of bartending for the week ahead as the bars are so busy that they need two bartenders working at a time.

Jacque meets a clerk from the Fort Langley Hudson's Bay trading post who askes him to come and work at that fort until he is ready to continue gold hunting. Jacque sees it as an excellent chance to make money to replace his part of the food supply in the future. He will take the canoe to Fort Langley and come back to us after a week.

Seph, Mike, and I will sleep in the tent, and I will help Mean Mike if he needs it. If he doesn't need much care, I will see if I can find some work, for most of my money has been spent on the canoe and food supplies and my own supplies for finding gold. Some will drink, gamble, and spend their last cent on having a good time. I prefer to work if there is a job to be had.

CHAPTER 7
Biding Our Time

FOLLOWING HIS TRIP to the doctor's, Mean Mike is too sick to argue about anything. His pounding head and blurred sight make him ready to rest and lie quiet. He cannot remember how he hit his head on the pistol or the ground. His speech is slurred, he feels dizzy and has ringing in his ears, but most of all, he is drained of energy and lies in his cot in exhaustion. I 'm trying to check in on Mike, but I've been employed by the doctor to help him deal with his constant lineup of patients and collect the five-dollar fee before the doctor sees them as patients.

I got my job because I do not take no for an answer if I believe I need one. I went to the doctor about Mean Mike several times the day after we brought him back to rest in the tent. The doctor quickly got frustrated at my dogged visits with questions about Mike's condition. After the third visit, the doctor said that I was annoying the hell out of him. About the fifth time I showed up, he said, "You may as well be a thorn in the flesh to others, as well as me. How would you like to work for me in the afternoons?" I readily agreed.

He decided that I'm to ask people why they want to see the doctor. I will then make a list of their symptoms and keep track of who gets in to see him next. The doctor has a nurse to help him, but she's busy with bandaging and helping with things like operations, gunshot wounds, stabbings, and caring for those too sick to leave the doctor's care. It's only for a week or so that I will be working for the doctor, but he calls me Mr. Brown. I've been called Nothing Brown for so long that Mr. Brown is extraordinary, but I like it.

Mean Mike is very slowly recovering. A bump on the head can be far more dangerous than we knew. We miss the solid good sense of Jacque, but Seph seems content to wait with Mike and me and is ready to help until we move on to find gold. He is quiet and not quick to speak his mind. Now that he is our partner, he still remains reluctant to share what he's thinking or his past.

Seph's story is this: "Nothing Brown sees me as quiet and private. I don't want to let the others know I own nothing but my smile and the clothes on my back. I'm out of money and not sorry our rush for gold has presently stalled. Mean Mike, Jacque, and Nothing Brown don't know that I started with very little money and it has long since vanished. I have never been so glad to be bartending afternoons to midnights for some money to my name.

"Gold fever holds everyone here at New Westminster, even bartenders, as everyone gets paid at the end of each day. It's understood that anyone may be gone to search for gold at any time. I'm part of the temporary workforce of bartenders, but it is good for me because there is no running a tab. I get no free drinks, and drinks are expensive, so I have been keeping sober and able to pocket my money.

"When I was young, it was fun to bartend. It seemed I was part of a great party. I enjoyed throwing out drunks and holding my own in the fights and brawls that came my way. Then being the muscle for the owner was no longer fun. The fights were hurting more, and I began to enjoy the liquor too much myself. Work was full of hangovers, my pay was always going on my tab, and my tab never got paid.

"I am no longer young and have little to show for my life so far. Many are like me here, as what you see is all there is, and finding gold is our only chance of getting rich. The four of us make the right combination of age and youth, experience, and daring. We see that our personal success is tied up with the strength of our group. Two can be better than one, and four can cut the unknown down to good odds for us all.

"Working at the saloon, I hear how there are plenty of officials from England here and how the newly formed Crown Colony of British Columbia is being established because of the gold rush. Governor Douglas is at Victoria, but a capital city is to take shape here at New Westminster. The word from the many American gold seekers like myself is that the British will always claim the whole world for their empire.

"It's obvious the British do and will run things here and claim authority over every stone, tree, mountain, and lake. Since gold has been found, the British Crown wants this slice of wilderness in their hands. I do like the British stress on law and order. There is no decent life without law and order, and I feel that there is a sense of that, especially here, and it was also evident at Victoria.

"There's lots of talk about a judge here from England ready to administer justice throughout the colony, including mining camps and the places growing up around the gold strikes. He will hold his courtroom in a tent or clearing. He is a man of stature and talent. He is an opera singer as well as an artist who may draw sketches of the witnesses in his court. He wears his judge's robes and wig wherever he holds his court. As a bartender, I'm told if an imposing man six feet five inches tall is at the bar with a black mustache, he well may be Judge Begbie ready for several drinks. It seems administrating colonial law and order is thirsty work.

"As a bartender, I would usually say that everyone at a saloon is thirsty for a drink and then another and more, or for some companionship, or cards, or for serious gambling, or sex if the salon girls are business-minded! Throw in a little music of a fiddle or a piano, some pickled eggs, some hard cheese and stale crackers and a fistfight or two, and everyone is glad to be there and not ready to go home.

"Here at New Westminster, with the gold rush on everyone's mind, drinking doesn't satisfy folks and their thirst for gold. Cards, companionship, gambling, and even sex are second places to the news of new gold strikes and where folks need to be to get in on the gold. I sometimes wonder if getting gold will satisfy people, but more importantly, will it satisfy me?

"I think of the words of King Solomon that everything is meaningless, like a dog chasing its tail. Is being in a gold rush like chasing the wind? If much wisdom brings much sorrow, will much gold bring much grief? Mean Mike wants a clear head and a chance at being healthy again. When is being healthy ever enough for us? I think of questions that have no answers. I think a lot because bartenders are paid to listen, not to talk. When Mean Mike is feeling good, he is a talker, but now he is a thinker on his cot. Less talk from Mean Mike is no hardship for me, but that doesn't mean I do not like him. He is a boiling pot in our group bubbling over in both action and chatter. Mike's excitement is contagious in our group. Since Mean Mike is not talking, his mind will be exploding in thoughts."

—

I don't mind sharing my thoughts as Mean Mike, the talker. Here I am, forced into fuzzy thinking here in our tent. All I'm doing is lying on my bed, trying to get well. I'm not mean or ready to fight as the time drags on with my head spinning. I'm feeling feeble in both my body and my mind. My headaches that last day after day scare me. I am like a helpless wee baby laid out on a cot because I am sick in the head. Whoever heard of their brain swelling? I suppose it is proof I have one, but when will I get back to normal? The doctor says that head injuries take time to heal, but will the others continue to wait for me until I'm better? Nothing Brown talks of working for the doctor and the endless patients needing help. Sometimes the doctor has Nothing Brown helping with the doctoring of patients. Cleaning wounds, applying simple bandages, boiling instruments in water, and a host of jobs beyond greeting those wanting to see the doctor. Nothing Brown does have a way of making me feel better. Being sick makes me feel depressed, but Nothing Brown gives me hope and helps me to believe it's just for a short time.

Jacque came to see us yesterday after being gone a week to Fort Langley. The week has been a rainy one. The Fraser is high and dangerous for canoes in areas further upriver from Fort Langley. He felt he would like to work there a week longer to give the river a chance to calm down. I thought he was being kind to me. I'm still having trouble with balance and getting back to normal. I'm better than I was, but still not fully right in my head. Nothing Brown and Seph agreed with Jacque that another week would be good to wait until the river was less dangerous. I feel that after another week, I'll be back to normal or close enough to get on with the gold search. Jacque, Seph, and Nothing Brown all seem to be glad to work for a second week, which is good for me too.

CHAPTER 8

A Baby Captivity

THIS SECOND WEEK of rest finds me stronger and clearer in my mind. Dizziness and balance issues have mostly gone, and I'm feeling optimistic about getting fully well again. Seph works until late at night and sleeps past noon. Nothing Brown leaves at noon to work at the doctor's office. Today is Wednesday, and I'm feeling so good that I plan to walk with Nothing Brown to his work and then walk back to the tent.

We leave early to slowly walk since it's the first time I'm going out and about. It is muddy because of the unusually wet stretch of weather here. Our muddy path to the doctor's place goes by an empty swampy area. As we pass the swamp, I see what looks like a bundle of clothes. I point it out to Nothing Brown, who thinks he hears some sound coming from the bundle. It is about ten or fifteen feet out in the swamp. Nothing Brown wades through ankle-high water, tall grass, and reeds to the packet. He finds in the bundle of rags a tiny, recently born baby crying weakly, wet and shivering.

He yells, "It's a tiny baby somebody has left here to die."

"Well, bring it out of there," I yell, and then I add, "we'll take it to the doctor."

Nothing Brown frees the baby from its bundle of rags and carries the baby back to the path like he is afraid of it.

"Give it here," I say to Nothing Brown, as I've had lots of practice with babies, being the oldest of thirteen children. Me ma didn't care that I was a boy because she was overrun with children younger than me, so she insisted I help her with all my brothers and sisters even when they were babies.

Nothing Brown is very willing to pass the tiny little soul to my care. The wee baby is shivering and making the smallest of whimpering sounds. I open my shirt and put the poor tiny baby next to my heart, wrap my shirt around it, and hold it to me to warm it.

Nothing Brown runs ahead, so the doctor will be ready to examine the baby when I get there with it. The doctor takes the baby from me, and removes the wet rag it is dressed in. He and the nurse gently bathe the baby in warm water, checking it, quickly drying it, and wrapping it in a little blanket.

"What do ya think about the baby?" I ask the doctor.

The doctor bluntly says, "It is a Chinese baby a few days old. It's very weak. It will probably die. We will try her with a little milk and see if she will nurse from a bottle. If she nurses even a little, we will send her home with you. You can keep her warm and safe, feed her, and wait. She will either live or die. My guess is that she will die within a day or two."

"Why would this baby be left to die? Is the baby sick or something?" Nothing Brown asks the doctor.

"The baby doesn't appear to be sick other than suffering from being abandoned in a slough. I can't say for sure, but I have heard that the Chinese do not always value female babies and sometimes leave them to die when born. It may or may not be the truth. You can certainly ask the Chinese for there are many of them here for the gold rush," the doctor answers.

The nurse has been trying the baby with a bottle, and the baby does suckle a little.

"This is a good sign, so take the baby home and care for her. We will send more milk for the bottle with Mr. Brown when he returns from work," the doctor tells me.

So, I walk home with the wee baby in my arms, thinking my ma would be saying to me, "Stop your complaining, Mike. It is only a helpless baby, and that baby will love you more than you will ever love it."

When I arrive home with the baby, Seph is amazed.

"A tad young for searching for gold seems to me," he says but insists on holding the wee baby. I can tell he's handled babies before and ain't afraid the baby will break like Nothing Brown.

"Did ya come from a big family like me, and did you need to help care for baby brothers or sisters?" I ask Seph.

"No," he says as he kisses the baby's forehead, "I had a son and daughter, but they died with their mother in a fire," he adds simply. Then he smiles and says to me, "A baby is a powerful little creature, and this baby will steal your heart, Mean Mike."

I ask Seph, "Will ya watch her and try to get her to nurse from the bottle? I need a rest before ya leave for work." Seph nods, yes.

I lay down on my cot and say, "This first walk has left me a little dizzy and tired," and I fall to sleep.

———

I, Nothing Brown, realize that when it comes to babies, I know just about nothing concerning the care of them. When I arrive at the tent after work at the doctor's office, with more milk, Mean Mike is rocking the baby back and forth in his arms. The baby is fussy, and Mean Mike hands the baby to me. My lack of experience with babies has me feeling anxious, but then he places her in my arms, and she stares at me with tiny eyes that see into my soul. At least that is how it seems to me. The baby senses someone new holding her and my calmness grows, which surprises me, and I feel very peaceful with her in my arms. I even begin to feel sleepy. I guess the baby does too, for she falls asleep right in my arms. It feels perfect to hold her as she sleeps.

It is now the end of the second week that we have been waiting for Mean Mike to get well. He is almost okay again. We have been so busy with the tiny baby that the last part of the week has gone by like a flash of lightning. Jacque cannot believe we have a baby in our midst when he returns from Fort Langley. The doctor tells us that our little angel will die soon, and we keep praying and hoping that he is wrong.

Jacque feels we should've taken her to a priest for baptism. We aren't aware that there is one at New Westminster, but there could be. Jacque takes the baby in his arms, blessing her. Making the sign of the cross, he says, "In the name of the Father, the Son, and the Holy Spirit." He leaves to see if he can find a priest. He is hardly gone, and the baby dies in Mean Mike's arms. Simply makes a tiny gasp and stops breathing.

Mean Mike and Seph are overcome with grief and both cry loudly, unable to stop, and I have a lump in my throat so that I cannot speak. After a few minutes, I take a shovel intending to search to see if there is a graveyard in this place.

Before I can leave, a very tall man approaches the tent looking for Seph. Seph introduces the man as Judge Begbie. He and the judge have spoken together at the saloon. The judge knows we plan to leave soon for Fort Langley and from there on up the Fraser to search for gold. The judge needs to hold court at Fort Langley and wants to know if he can travel in our canoe with us to Fort Langley.

He is quick to see our present distress. He is respectful of our grief, and Jacque returns, having been unable to find a priest and hangs his head in sadness at the baby's death.

The judge knows of a burial place, and so we proceed with shovel and baby to an area with wooden crosses. We find the end of the row of graves and dig a hole for the tiny baby. Seph has brought from the saloon an empty wooden whiskey box in which we place the baby wrapped in her blanket.

The judge offers to say a few words and sing a hymn. Once the baby's body is lowered in the ground. His words are simply: "The Lord has given this baby; the Lord has taken her away. May God hold her soul in his hands. Amen." Then he sings the psalter: "Praise God, from whom all blessings flow; Praise Him all creatures here below; Praise Him above, ye heavenly host; Praise Father, Son, and Holy Ghost. Amen."

We cover the baby's body with dirt, and the judge says, "Ashes to Ashes, dust to dust in the hope of the resurrection of the dead to eternal life. Amen."

The judge returns with us to our tent, and we tell him he is welcome to canoe with us to Fort Langley, and we will leave the next day. He will be ready, he assures us, and he leaves with our thanks for being part of our burial service for our baby.

CHAPTER 9

The Administrator of Justice

MORNING COMES WITH a reluctant sun, and the four of us are feeling empty without our tiny baby. How that baby could mean so much to us in such a short time is beyond us. We are glad to be leaving New Westminster behind us. We are standing at the shore with our canoe loaded, waiting for the first chief justice of the Crown Colony of British Columbia. Like a breath of fresh air, Judge Begbie comes down to the river, ready to travel with us to Fort Langley. We don't know what to expect: Will the judge be a friendly fellow? Will he row along with the rest of us? Will he treat as servants or inferiors?

"My name is Matthew, and that's all that I want to be called as we paddle this canoe together," the judge instructs us as we leave from the shore. He is at home in our canoe. He is an excellent oarsman joining in rowing readily. We are paddling against the current, and the river is higher than usual due to the rainy weather. We all paddle hard to make progress. Matthew offers to tell us about himself. He feels that he knows about each of us from talking with Seph at the saloon. We are eager to learn his story and encourage the judge to tell us about himself.

He says, "My father was an army colonel, and I was born on a British ship going to the island of Mauritius. It is in the Indian

Ocean. We returned to England when I was seven, and I was edu-cated there. I studied mathematics and the classics at the University of Cambridge. My heart at university was in singing, acting, playing chess, rowing, and tennis for which there are no degrees granted. Rowing is a team sport there, not a way to travel rivers into the wilderness. After Cambridge, I completed my law degree, and I had a law practice in London until I was offered the position of chief justice of the new colony of British Columbia. It was at Fort Langley that I was sworn into office as the new colony of British Columbia was proclaimed there on November 19, 1858.

"I accepted the position because I am an adventurer and believe in the rule of law wherever there is a British colony. I wanted to travel with you to Fort Langley to understand all I can about the people I'm to judge here in British Columbia. I hope to learn what Jacque can teach me from his years in the Hudson's Bay Company. He can also help me to learn about the Indians. From you three Americans, I hope to determine if you will stay if you find gold or return home. I can learn much from each of you as we travel together. I also hope to beat you at chess or cards, sing with you, and see the best way to build a night camp in the wilderness beside a river."

We begin to see a man of substance in Judge Begbie, who already has much awareness about the colony. The judge asks Jacque if his perception of the Hudson's Bay Company is correct. He says, "It is my understanding that the Crown gave the company the charter or control of the colony of Vancouver Island and this mainland years ago. The company controlled the whole area with a series of fur trading posts. The white population as employees of the company was low, and they often married native women so that there has been a mixture of the two. I believe that, until now, the Hudson's Bay employees with their mixed families have had great power and influ-ence, but the influx of gold seekers has changed everything. Those arriving shun the mixing of white and native. The old is crumbling about us. The past emphasis on furs has now become gold. Aren't the Hudson's Bay posts now centers of supplies for the many seeking gold?"

Jacque nods his head and says, "It's the sad truth."

The judge addresses us: "Is it true that the American and Chinese gold seekers have little respect for the Hudson's Bay Company or the natives that are here as you come here to search for gold?"

Mean Mike, back in good health, says to the judge, "I've no problem with the Hudson's Bay Company for gettin' supplies. No British officials or no Indians better try to keep me from searching for gold in this here wilderness."

"I will interfere with your gold search if you murder, steal, rob, or cause other trouble," replies the judge.

"I reckon that's fair enough," Mean Mike answers.

Seph also says to the judge, "I think that Americans like me see the natives as part of the frontier and wilderness. We don't see them as having a true and legal right to the land because it is wilderness. We consider the natives as dangerous, even deadly, needing to adjust to the ways of the whites or perish."

"Some of us Americans do respect the natives and seek to help them to become one with the whites. Missionaries share their faith and educate the Indians in our ways. They seek understanding between them and us," I say to the judge.

"Do you believe that we too need to learn of the Indian faith and ways of life, Nothing Brown?" the judge asks me.

"I think we must learn enough of their ways and language to be able to talk to them and teach them," I answer.

"Would you join me in studying Indian languages? I am working at speaking the Shuswap and Chilcotin tongues."

"I can only answer you honestly, no," I say.

Jacque says, "I can speak several Indian tongues. I have French-Canadian blood as well as native blood. All blood is red, all bleed and die in a fight for control. The company, the Crown, the settlers, the gold seekers, the fur traders, and the natives will never control the land as it is a gift. A gift that never belongs to you. You can claim it and defend it, but it is only yours in your mind. Native or white take nothing with them in death, neither land nor gold. We must look much further than ourselves in search of the giver of the gifts. Our search is for peace between everyone by sharing the land, water, food, or gold. They belong to all."

"Your Catholic roots run deep Jacque," the judge says.

"Maybe," Jacque answers.

"Tell us of Fort Langley, Jacque. What do you know of it?" the judge says to him.

"It is the busiest that I have ever seen," Jacque responds. "It has never been such a busy fort for fur pelts but a busy supply place of fish, potatoes, and cranberries for the company. The farmlands of Fort Langley have long made the fort a busy and prosperous center, but now with the cry for food for the gold seekers, the fort is doing business as never before. Back in 1832, the fort began with a handful of cows but added more through the years. That has led to supplying beef, with the salmon, and the cranberries. The demand for meat and fish is greater now than it ever has been. In a gold rush, you can live without gold, but you cannot live without food."

"Gold rushes are good for business, just ask Seph how the saloons prosper," the judge says to Jacque, who readily agrees.

Our canoe trip from New Westminster to Fort Langley continues full of talk, laughter, song, and high spirits, for the judge is a ready companion to each of us and our whole group. He inspires us because he is eager to embrace this entire new British colony to understand it, honor it as it is, and ensure that it has law and order by the authority given him by the Crown.

CHAPTER 10
Court Justice

WE INTENDED TO leave Judge Begbie at Fort Langley and continue up the Fraser in search of gold, but a circumstance stalled us there. Upon arrival at the fort, the judge asked us to stay and see him conduct his court the next day. One of the cases he was to hear had to do with a charge against an American, John Russ, for assaulting a native man. The judge wanted Jacque to be there to help interpret for him if he could not manage on his own. The judge had been such a great traveling companion that we decided to stay for his court the next day.

Judge Begbie wore his robe and wig to preside over his courtroom, held in the dining hall at the main house at the fort. There were five cases to be tried: the first three dealing with drunkenness were dispatched quickly. The fourth case surprised Jacque, Seph, Mean Mike, and me because the person on trial was named Wilfred Magee. By his age, we decided it must be Old Man Magee that we had heard about from Ed.

The chief trader at the fort wanted Wilfred Magee banished from the fort and its surrounding area. Magee was charged with mischief and causing continuous disturbances. As the case was presented to the judge, we learned that gold seekers camped in tents around the

49

fort are customers of a big tent used as a saloon in the shadow of the fort walls. At the tent, Magee begged for money to buy his drinks. Unbeknown to Magee, some patrons placed their smallest coins in the hot coal pail, and then pulled the coins out with tongs, placing them on the bar. Then they would tell Magee to grab the penny or pennies, which he often did if he was drunk enough. His screams at picking up the hot pennies was a big joke to some in the saloon. Magee was also a singer and made some coins for his singing. The problem was that the more Magee drank, the more he invented words to his songs that caused laughter and fights.

By the time of his court date, Magee has been in jail for four days because his last song in the saloon referred to Mae, the most popular lady of the bar. Mae responded to the song by threatening to wring Magee's neck, and she tried to catch him as he crawled under the bar to get away from her anger. In doing so, the bar was knocked over, and it was full of whiskey bottles that fell off it. The bottles got grabbed by thirsty customers close by. Others fought and wrestled with those who caught the bottles to get the bottles away from them. A brawl resulted. The saloon owner wanted Magee hung. The constable wanted Magee banished because he disturbed the business of the fort as well as the saloon.

Judge Begbie asked Wilfred Magee if he sang opera in the saloon, and Magee said that he sang bass. The judge smiled and asked Magee to sing a song that he used in the big tent. Wilfred Magee, thin, ravaged by age and drink, sang in a clear and fine voice:

"Alas, my love you do me wrong,

To cast me off discourteously

For I have loved you well and long

Delighting in your company."

The judge stopped him before he could continue the chorus of "Greensleeves" and said to Magee, "You sing an exceptional old English ballad. Are you English?"

"Yes, Your Honor."

"Are the charges against you true?" the judge asked.

"Yes, Your Honor, I have loved my liquor way too long and well, and I'm its fool now. There is no hope for me," Magee replied.

"Nonsense," Judge Begbie replied. "I know a group of men heading for Fort Hope and Yale. They have no liquor with them, and you will dry out with them and will have a chance to start over." The judge looked to us and said, "Gentlemen, can Mr. Magee travel with you to Fort Hope and Yale?" We looked at each other in surprise and were hesitant to answer yes.

"If he runs away from you as you travel, so be it. His future is in your hands," the judge said, and we nodded yes with reluctance.

The judge said, "Mr. Magee, you will leave this fort and area by canoe with those gentlemen sitting there by the wall. You are fined five dollars for mischief and disorderly conduct when drunk. Do you have any money to pay the fine?"

"No, Your Honor," Magee answered.

"I will pay his fine," I offered.

"Thank you, Mr. Brown, you may come and pay the clerk now before I hear the last case. While you do that, Mr. Magee and I will sing the chorus to the lovely ballad 'Greensleeves.'" They both sang the chorus well, and I paid the fine.

The last case was against a John Russ, an American with an abusive attitude. He was charged with assault against a native man. John Russ was arrested by the constable when natives came to him about a fight in progress. He found John Russ beating on a native man who was bleeding on the ground. The natives informed the constable that the white man had grabbed the native man's teenage

51

daughter, and the man had hindered the white man from molesting his daughter. The natives felt if the constable had not come, the white man would have beaten the girl's father to death.

The judge had John Russ swear on the Bible to tell the truth as God as his witness. Then he asked John Russ, "Did you grab the teenage Indian girl?"

"Just a little grab is all," John Russ answered.

"Had you been drinking?" asked the judge.

"Hell, yes, or I would've touched her," Russ answered. "She would've liked it if her old man wasn't there," he added.

"What makes you think so?" the judge asked.

"She is an Indian, and they all want to be with a white man," Russ added.

"Did you fight with and beat up her father?" asked the judge.

"Well, I didn't know he was her old man," Russ said.

"Would you have backed off if you knew the man was her father?" asked the judge.

"No, because they're Indians and don't count. Why would you side with Indians against me, a white man? You won't be judge long if you are an Indian lover," Russ snarled.

The judge said, "You could be right, Mr. Russ. You are excused from giving your testimony now. Go wait by the constable."

The judge asked the native man who had been beaten up to give his side of the story. The man spoke a native dialect that Jacque understood. The judge was able to get some of the man's testimony on his own, and Jacque helped fill in the gaps in understanding the man's story.

After hearing from three native witnesses and the constable, Judge Begbie sentenced John Russ to three years in prison for assault but gave him the option to return to the USA and stay there instead.

John Russ agreed to return home. The judge said he would arrange a constable escort to the border for Russ. Russ's friends were outraged at the verdict, but Jacque and I were pleased with it, and Mean Mike, Seph, and Wilfred Magee did not voice an opinion about the decision.

Judge Begbie treated us to supper, including Wilfred Magee, and he and the judge sang songs familiar to them both, well into the evening.

CHAPTER 11
Ward of the Court

OLD MAN MAGEE came to us after his trial, having survived four days of sobriety in jail. He presented himself to us as a friendly and sensible old fellow. He claimed that drink made him act like an ass, but there was a twinkle in his old eyes and grin that spoke of mischief in his heart. Jacque was able to get him a blanket from the fort, which we all chipped in to buy for him. Other than the clothes on his back and the one blanket we gave him, his earthly goods were contained in a small canvas sack that was three-quarters empty. The judge arranged for a little provision of food for Magee to get him to Fort Hope or Yale, depending on his appetite. Old Man Magee seemed genuinely pleased with both the food and blanket and was ready to travel with us upriver.

The old man was up and ready to start while the rest of us could hardly get our eyes open the morning following his trial. We set off in our canoe with a sense of excitement and a touch of gold fever. At last, it seemed, that we were closing in on the places that gold had been found along the river before us. We were frustrated that the river was still high in August because of rainy weather. Often by August, the river was at its lowest level, and the gravel bars with gold in them uncovered for gold panning.

We had hardly gotten away from Fort Langley when we had to pull into the shore. Our canoe was taking on water, and it wasn't easy to see why. The mystery ended when we had the canoe unloaded on the shore, and we discovered someone had shot three holes in the bottom of the canoe. There was one bullet hole at the front, one at the middle, and one at the back of the boat. It seemed someone was carrying a grudge against Old Man Magee or us. Maybe it seemed we were too friendly with Judge Begbie. Was it the friends of John Russ?

The holes were not large but needed to be filled. Jacque was sure he could fix the three holes with some pine sap, especially if he could find a tree with a buildup of pine sap goo on the outside of a tree limb or trunk. We needed to stop and camp while Jacque, Seph, and Mean Mike went in search of pine tree sap. The trees nearest our camp on the shore were willow, cedar, and oak. Old Man Magee warned the men that the forest could swallow up people and never spit them out, so they should mark a trail. Jacque agreed with him and promised that they would return as soon as possible.

With the three other men gone hunting pine goo, I set to work putting our tent up and gathering wood for our fire for cooking. I was also on the lookout for any ripe raspberries growing wild. When I returned with an armload of wood, Old Man Magee was fishing with line and hook that he carried in his canvas bag. I was both surprised and pleased to see three nice-sized salmon near him. Magee was glad to be providing food for us, and he was singing, making up songs and tunes as he fished in joy. When I inspected the caught salmon, Magee sang a song about my name with a slightly altered tune to "Clementine." I had to listen to my song:

"Oh, my darling, oh, my darling
Oh, my darling, Nothing Brown
You are lost and gone forever
Dreadful sorry, Nothing Brown

"In a colony, in a river, miner 59er
Fell in water, well above his ears
Drown a Quaker, met his Maker
All his partners shed sad tears."

I was smiling as he sang the song, and together we sang the song a couple of times in fun. Old Man Magee then asked if I could read and write, for he wanted to have a poem of his written out in his poetry book. He said that his hands were old and shaky, and his handwriting hardly legible. I said that my writing was clear and readable and that if Magee gave me his book, I would write out his poem for him, with his pen and ink. I tended his fishing line while he found and produced a small black book, pen, and ink from his canvas bag.

So, on that bright sunny morning, Old Man Magee fished and caught salmon, while I wrote his poem in his book. To this day, I have no idea if his poem has any merit, but I liked it and made a copy for myself with his blessing. I shared his poetry with the others, and they thought it did not rhyme enough. It spoke truth to me as it was not long or hard to understand, it was called simply,

The Fraser.
Dirty brown river hurrying along
Filled with mean pride and spirit.
Treacherous water, tempting with hidden gold.

Homegrown, back in mountain peaks
A razor cutting rock and pushing land
Bending and stretching in long winding flow
To empty in the ocean far below.

Scorning us foolish folk — here
To poke and choke out your gold.
You laid the snare to get rich
Ready to watch us die trying.

By the time the poem was written, Old Man Magee had a total of seven excellent salmon for our supper. He might have caught even more but was interrupted in his fishing by gunshots. Since the shots were coming from a canoe on the river heading towards us on the shore, we took cover behind some large oak tree trunks.

As the canoe advanced, we could see the person in the middle of the canoe was the one with a rifle. The boat was powered by two paddlers, one in front and one at the rear. When the canoe came to the shore itself, the paddlers stayed with the boat. The person with the rifle was a woman in men's clothes.

She came ashore yelling, "Wilfred Magee show your sorry self, or I'll hunt you down, you cowardly dog."

Old Man Magee whispered to me behind the tree trunk, "Story of my life, women won't leave me alone." He yelled from behind the trunk, "I know it's you, Mae, and I have told you for the last time that I will not marry you. You can shoot me, but I'll be no good to you as a husband if I'm dead."

"I don't want to live without you, Magee. Quit making me beg you to marry me," the woman answered.

"Be honest, Mae, people like my singing, and you like the money I bring in the saloon as the old drunk that is good to laugh at or abuse. I'm good for business is why you want me. I have told you that I'm already married," Magee said.

"You're a liar; you're not married! You can't be because I want you for my husband. You clean up good and look handsome and dignified in a suit," Mae said. "We could make a nice respectable couple in Victoria," she added.

"No, I'm not going to live off your money and pretend to be respectable. If you want me, you will have to wait for me until I find gold and stop being a drunk. Do you want a real honest-to-God respectable husband?" Magee challenged.

"I'm getting too old, Magee, to be waiting for anyone. My looks are fading, and the time is coming when I won't even be able to give my companionship away. What are the chances that you will find gold and quit drinking?" she asked.

"I have found some gold already, but I wasted it on drink. I could find more gold, but will I waste it again and remain a drunk? You would be better off with someone else, Mae, for it would be a huge gamble to trust me to become a respectable and sober husband. Cut your losses, send me away gladly, and let me come back to you, if you still want me, as I should be, not as a lie," Magee answered.

"I promise you this, Magee, if you come back to me, whether rich or poor, drunk or sober, I will love you. I'm going to gamble on you. Now get out here and kiss me good-bye if you love me too," she said, crying.

Magee ran out to Mae, and they kissed so passionately and with such length, I wasn't sure what would happen next. They both separated their kiss after an eternity, with tears in their eyes. Magee whispered, "I'm coming back to you."

Mae said, "I'm betting on you with all my heart." Then she climbed into the canoe, and she never looked back as her boat headed for Fort Langley.

I said to Magee, "I think you are a lucky man to have that lady waiting for you."

He said, "It sure gives me someone to live for besides my sorry self."

CHAPTER 12
More Visitors Than Wanted

THE THREE PINE sap collectors returned early evening with goo enough to plug the three holes in the canoe. They were thrilled to have plenty of salmon to fry for supper. We fried the seven salmon with the intent of having leftovers for the morning's breakfast, but the salmon disappeared in the evening meal like it was a mere bite for each of us.

We were all delighted that Old Man Magee was such a good fisherman. He did not share with the others about Mae's visit during the day, and I did not mention it either. It was his personal business to share if he cared to with the others. We all went to bed early to be ready for an early start in the morning, and we decided to take turns keeping a guard during the night.

I offered to keep watch first. Mean Mike was to be next after me, then Seph, followed by Old Man Magee. Jacque would begin the watch the next night. It was a night the guards awoke our camp to visitors.

I had hardly begun my watch when a bear came lumbering into camp, perhaps smelling fried salmon. I woke everyone, and we all got our guns and moved back to give the bear free range through our camp. It sniffed the campfire ashes, shuffled over to the tent doorway where Old Man Magee had been sleeping and had left his shoes and socks to air out during the night. The bear had a whiff of the footwear, threw its head back, and swatted the boots several feet and wandered away from the tent and down to the river where it began following the shoreline upriver. After the bear scare, everyone kept their gun beside them in case the bear returned to have one of us for a midnight snack.

It seemed like Mean Mike was going to have a peaceful watch, but Mike noticed the bushes moving and went to check to make sure it wasn't the bear returning, only to disturb a skunk. The irate skunk proceeded to spray Mike, who yelled and cursed at the skunk so loudly that everyone sleeping was awakened to a terrible smell. Realizing it was Mike fouling the air, we would not let him near the tent and forced him to soak himself in the river, which he said was ice cold.

The smell was so strong and evil that we set our biggest pot to boil and threw Mike's smelly clothes in the boiling water. To the boiling water we added a piece of soap, some salt, a little chunk of chewing tobacco, Old Man Magee's socks, and some cologne that Seph had. After Mean Mike had washed with soap three times in the river, he was forced to sit naked by the fire, in the hope the stink might lessen or get covered by campfire smoke.

It didn't seem Seph would need to keep watch with Mean Mike sitting naked by the fire watching his clothes boiling in a pot. Yet, Seph said he wasn't sure he could sleep in the stink, so he kept watch only to find an hour later that two canoes were heading our way on the river. He woke us and warned us all to stay awake with our guns ready but to keep out of sight.

The two canoes floated in quietly, and eight men came sneaking up the shore. The strong smell of skunk had them coughing and covering their noses. After some gagging and choking, the leader announced loudly, "We are here to teach you, the friends of the judge, what happens to Indian lovers. John Russ was our friend."

Mean Mike had been watching them, and he yelled, "Don't come closer, these guys are crazy. They trapped a skunk and had me open the trap. That skunk sprayed me, and now they're boiling the skunk in this pot. Remember that old guy from the trial? There's nothing left but his socks!" Mean Mike picked up a stick for the fire and fished Old Man Magee's socks out of the pot. "It is some sort of insane British justice that they carry out for that judge. Your friend is lucky he got sent back to American soil."

"We're going to teach all of you a lesson. Where are the others?" their ringleader snarled.

"They're off hanging the old man's dead body on a tree. They've about a dozen Indians with them. They're into some sort of Indian bloodletting ceremony. If you guys take off, let me come with you. If they catch you here, you'll end naked and covered in skunk spray like me," Mean Mike lied to them.

"I think you're bullshitting us. We're coming in to beat your Indian-loving ways right out of you and the others. I think they're hiding," the leader said.

Seph watching and listening from tree cover whistled loudly and yelled: "Hurry up! We've company, and there's plenty for scalping!" He fired his gun into the air. Then Jacque made an Indian war cry from the side of the tent that made the hair stand up on my neck. The friends of John Russ did not stay on the shore but jumped into their canoes and took off as fast as they could paddle. We each shot one shot after the attackers. We did not want to wound or kill anyone; just get rid of them.

We put tea on and sat around marveling at the night that had happened to us. The wind picked up, and we took Mike's clothes and Magee's socks out of the pot and hung them to dry. Mean Mike was brought other clothes he had in the tent and he put them on.

It was hard to tell if he smelled less like a skunk because skunk odor hung in the air and burnt our sinuses. Old Man Magee was amazed that his socks withstood the boiling as he could not remember how many years it was since they were washed.

CHAPTER 13
Endless Company and Competition

LOOKING BACK ON it now, our canoe trip to Fort Hope was the end of our easy travel and companionship. The closer we came to Fort Hope, the higher the number of people we experienced searching for gold. On the Fraser, we found not only an endless flow of fellow gold seekers, but they often had rockers.

Old Man Magee had suggested that we would gain more gold if we had a rocker with the five of us working together. We had to agree with him that gold panning was a staple of discovering gold but was often time-consuming. It could be a tedious time of carefully moving the water in your pan, removing large stones, and breaking up dirt with your fingers, while patiently moving the water in circles to search for gold in the bottom of your pan.

With a rocker, two or three people could be working the machine while others were gold panning. A rocker was like a baby's cradle that could be rocked back and forth using a handle. A shovelful of dirt, gravel, sand, and water was placed into a box on top of the rocker. The box had holes in it. Underneath the box was a slopping round surface called a slide or apron. As the rocker was rocked back and forth, the finer gold and sand would wash through the holes in the top of the box and be caught by ridges and canvas on the apron.

With so many other gold seekers beside us, we were into a crowded race to get as much gold as we could in often a limited area on the river bars or banks.

When we reached Murderer's Bar below Fort Hope, the number of people panning for gold on the bar was staggering. It was late in the day when we reached it, and we decided to camp on the shore near the bar and see if we could do any panning on or near the bar in the morning. The word was that all the bars from Fort Hope to Fort Yale were being furiously worked by deadly earnest gold seekers, ready to fight anyone who got in their way. The big speculation was about the bars beyond Fort Yale. They were said to be richer in gold, but when would they appear again as the water was too high yet to find them.

Mean Mike said, "We've entered a serious place where everyone is so intent on finding gold that a person can get shot for saying hello."

Old Man Magee said, "It is a world made up of men named Ed, who have their hearts set on all the gold they can get, and it will never be enough."

Seph suggested that we look out for each other as never before for many of our fellow gold hunters were honest, but there would be those ready to steal from those celebrating success. He counseled that we should show frustration and disappointment as much as possible even if we found gold nuggets the size of apples. Don't let on that you have found gold if you do. Keep a poker face.

I said, "We should place whatever gold we find together. That way, we will not be comparing who found more and or less. It will keep resentment and jealousy down. Every two weeks or every week, we will split the gold in five ways."

Mean Mike said to me, "I'm not sure what ya mean."

I told Mike, "We should be partners splitting whatever we find equally, one for all and all for one."

Jacque said that we could try it for our first week and see if everyone was satisfied with the partnership. He liked the idea that we were in our gold search together rather than every person for himself.

Everyone was willing to try our partnership for a week, and it was voted on that Jacque would be given all the gold that we each collected as we gathered it. We did not sleep much that first night beside Murderer's Bar, as we knew that now our search for gold was getting real.

We had camped beside Murderer's Bar on the shore of the Fraser, and we decided that we would keep one of us in camp during the day, and it would be a place of rest for us as we worked the bar. The word was that there were thirty bars ahead of us on the Fraser from Hope to Fort Yale. We felt that we would try each one and use a rocker on each once we had bought one.

Luck was with us when we went to the bar in the morning. There was a significant group of Chinese in one area of the bar, and a small space beside the Chinese was vacant. It seemed during the night the two miners who worked there had a drunken argument, and they shot each other. They had been taken to Fort Hope for doctoring, and when we negotiated with the Chinese to buy a rocker from them, they were glad to have us beside them on the bar. The price we arrived at was half of the gold we found for two days. A pretty little Chinese girl would watch our panning and work with the rocker and take whatever gold we discovered that was their share.

The rocker worked well, and our panning was profitable. It seemed sad to give half the gold we found to the Chinese girl, but she had a pretty smile and eyes. She did not speak English, but it seemed she understood every word we said to each other. The work was hard in that the panning was hard on the back and cold on the hands. Mean Mike and I had boots with us because we had looked for gold in California. The others had wet feet. That first day our enthusiasm was boundless.

We found that we were glad to be beside the Chinese, who were quiet workers intent on finding gold. The others on the bar who were mainly American, but with some British, Dutch, French, German, and Australian. They were a mixture of hard labor and a rowdiness of gambling, drunkenness, fistfights, and gunshots in the air or at each other. The first two days had all of us in a daze; we were all tired, for like the Chinese, we worked steadily, thrilled with every speck of gold we uncovered.

The third day on the bar had us as excited as boys smoking a corncob pipe behind the barn. The rocker was paid for, and all gold found was ours at last. In spite of Seph's caution that we keep our faces blank when finding gold, Mean Mike forgot when he found a wonderful nugget. He blurted out with all the clarity of loud thunderclap, "Slap my bare ass with all the heather in Scotland, look at this one, Nothing Brown."

The Chinese stopped working and looked at Mean Mike. The loud side of the bar also became dead quiet. All eyes were on Mean Mike, and I pulled his pan down to eye level and said, "Okay, Mikey, put the frog carefully in the water."

"Okay," Mean Mike said, like a hurt child, and he stepped into the river and emptied his pan in the water. He, of course, did it in such a way to catch the nugget in his hand.

He came back crying, "But, Nothing, I wanted that frog! When do I get to keep a frog?"

I whispered in his ear, "Good cover." The Chinese looked puzzled but quickly returned to their work. The others from the rowdy side of the bar shook their heads. Seph and Jacque said in embarrassment, "The boy is big, but he is slow."

Someone yelled from the thugs, "He ain't the only slow one here, so is Frenchy, he is just plain big and stupid." Then there erupted a fistfight that many seemed to enjoy as a break from looking for gold. After the fistfight, which Frenchy won, the day passed without incident.

After dark, three of us would be in camp on the shore while two stayed on the piece of the bar we were working. Old Man Magee would always cover the darkness to dawn with one of us. He would sing early in the night, and his beautiful voice would carry over the river. No one complained of his singing. During the day, he gathered wood and guarded our camp. He got in some fishing each day. He would trade the fish he caught with other miners for flour, sugar, tea, rice, or even some bacon or beans.

I said we were blessed, but my partners said that we were downright lucky. We had five very profitable days on Murderer's Bar. On the sixth day, two men with wounds that were bandaged, returned, and demanded we get off their spot on the bar. The Chinese confirmed that they were the ones working in our area until they shot each other. We didn't know if they had filed a claim, but we left as they ordered.

We proceeded to Fort Hope where the gold we have collected was split five ways between us by Jacque. It was not even a full week of searching for gold, but Seph, Jacque, and Old Man Magee needed boots. We needed to replenish food supplies. At the fort, we each stocked up on things we needed or wanted and have gold left over. After we got our supplies, we canoed past Fort Hope and found the next gravel bar on the river. We set up camp near it on the shore, and Seph, Jacque, and Mean Mike returned to Fort Hope for the evening. Jacque always had people he knew in the Hudson's Bay Company forts and would spend time with them when he had the chance. Mean Mike and Seph wanted to drink and spend time with the ladies. I thought of talking to the doctor at the fort, for in my mind I wanted to become a doctor after I had finished hunting gold, but I stayed behind at camp.

I was content to stay with Old Man Magee. He was serious about keeping sober for Mae. Magee had talked with an out-of-money gold seeker at the fort who wanted to sell his fiddle. Old Man Magee had bought it from him and began practicing with his violin.

He said, "To many, it is a fiddle, but to me, it is a violin." He was skillful at playing his violin. The evening passed quickly in the beautiful tunes that he coached out his instrument. He shared that he could also play the piano, but the violin was his first love.

Before morning, Seph and Jacque returned to camp with Mean Mike bruised and battered. Mike had not only got drunk but insisted on fist-fighting all takers. His only moment of real glory was when he beat Frenchy with a left hook. He won about as many fights as he lost. Son like father, we assumed.

Mean Mike did not have drinking, fighting, and ladies out of his mind when he partly sobered up the next morning. We were all a little surprised and saddened when Mike announced that he was packing his stuff and going back to Fort Hope to enjoy himself until he ran low on money, and then he would come up the Fraser to find us and partner with us again. Mike was the youngest in spirit among us and was a lively and likable lad. He was strong and a steady worker and rower, but he needed to live his life as he wanted. He wanted to spend his gold, and we watched him go, wishing he would stay with us instead.

CHAPTER 14

Attacks and Troubles

WE BEGAN WORK on the second gravel bar with a sense of a person missing. The second bar was much smaller than Murderer's Bar, and just a handful of Chinese were working it. They did not resist our effort to work the bar also, and for three days, we worked the bar beside Chinese workers with success. We decided after finishing early afternoon on the third day that it was time to move to the next bar on the Fraser.

I could not resist suggesting we go back to Fort Hope and have a look for Mean Mike in case he might have partied himself low on money and would be ready to join us again. Everyone was up for the idea, so we canoed back to Fort Hope, not wanting to move further upriver without checking on Mean Mike. When we reached Fort Hope, we split up searching the fort and settlement in hopes of finding him. We looked, but we could not find Mean Mike, and there were two stories about him.

The first story we all dismissed. It was that Mean Mike had gone off with the Chinese to trade firewater and rifles with the Indians. The second story seemed very unlikely to us also; it was that Frenchy and Mean Mike had gone to Fort Yale to join a militia to fight the Indians. We went back to camp stumped as to what Mean Mike was doing. We would have felt better if he had been there drunk and fighting, but to just disappear didn't sit well with any of us.

It was starting to get dark when we reached our camp and we set about starting the campfire so we could cook a bite of supper. Old Man Magee yelled from the door of the tent, "Come here and look, we've been robbed." He held up his arm and hand to motion us to come and see, an arrow struck him in the shoulder, and he crumpled backward into the tent. Seph pulled his pistol out and took a shot mostly into the dark. Jacque had his gun ready, and when he saw a movement at the side of the clearing, he shot at the movement. Nothing moved there again, so Seph and Jacque went about searching around the camp for Indians.

I went to the tent to check on Old Man Magee, who had passed out in pain. The arrow was not imbedded deeply in his shoulder, and I was able to pull it out without tearing the flesh any more than the arrow had already done. I bandaged his shoulder and made him as comfortable as I could. He seemed to be suffering from shock, and I was worried about him. It wasn't a deep wound, but would he be able to recover from it, I wondered.

Seph and Jacque called an all clear, and I went to them at the campfire. They too, were doubtful that Old Man Magee would be okay with an arrow wound. There was some hope because he had not lost a great deal of blood. A voice said, "Put your guns away; you already shot at me once." We turned in amazement to see Mean Mike ambling up to us as big as life!

"Where the hell did you come from?" Seph asked as he gave Mike a big bear hug that caught Mike by surprise.

"I followed you from the fort in my own little canoe. I was about to show myself to you when Old Man Magee yelled, and then you fired into the dark. I figured that since it was you, Seph, you'd shoot yourself and anyone but the Indians. I went around the back of the tent and came up to the edge of the bushes, and Jacque almost hit me with his shot, so I sat down undercover until it seemed you two trigger-happy boys were done firing your guns. I saw that it was a young Indian boy who shot his arrow on the run, good thing that his aim was slightly off. Still, he hit Magee, but maybe with not all the force of a full-grown brave would have had. I hope the old man is okay."

We all went to the tent to check on Old Man Magee and see what the Indians had stolen. They had taken any tobacco and liquor that was stashed in bedrolls or personal belongings. Everything was turned upside down and inside out in a search for any gold that might be found. Being a faithful Quaker, I came out best because I had no tobacco or alcohol to be stolen. We all kept any gold or money we had on our person. Jacque and Seph went to make tea and some supper while Mean Mike and I put Old Man Magee on my bedroll so it would be more comfortable for him.

Mean Mike said, "He's as light as you, Nothing Brown. He's nothing but skin and bones."

"Watch what you're saying, Mean Mike, or I'll box your ears tomorrow," Old Man Magee muttered. "When's supper? No wonder I don't weigh much," the old man said. Then his brow wrinkled in pain, and he whispered, "Let me rest till you bring my supper," then he drifted off into a painful slumber. We covered him with his blanket and left him to sleep.

"It is hard to keep a good man down," I said to Mike, nodding to Old Man Magee.

He said, "I hope you're right."

CHAPTER 15
Troubled Outlook

OLD MAN MAGEE was awake the next morning and insisted that he was well enough to move on to the next gravel bar. It was about a half-a-day canoe trip, and Magee emphasized that he was well enough, but that he couldn't do much paddling just yet. The distance was further than we imagined so that it was late afternoon when we spotted the next bar, which was a large one close to the right bank of the river. As we closed in, our blood ran cold as dead bodies lay across the gravel. Arrows buried in their bodies spoke of death by Indians. We headed for shore to see if there were miners' camps there and if there were any people left.

It seemed there had been camps, but all we could find were several spots that had once been campfires. We set up camp and got Old Man Magee lying down to rest. The more extended trip had him exhausted and a bit feverish. We decided the next thing we needed to do was bury the bodies rather than leave them to the river's mercy. Jacque and I sought a spot where we could dig in the earth, and we set about spading out as much dirt as we could in a square area. While we struggled to dig a big grave, Mean Mike and Seph carried the dead bodies from the bar, eight of them, to the grave site. They spelled us off, and between the four of us we dug a shallow, wide grave for the bodies. We covered the grave with dirt, and then some large river rocks and several fallen logs. We did not want wild animals to dig up and feed on the corpses.

It was close to midnight when we finished by the light of a big bonfire. We all felt that we needed to do it before anything else. We collapsed in exhaustion around the fire, feeling numb and somber. While Jacque prepared tea, I went to check on Old Man Magee, who had a higher fever, and it seemed his wound was infected. I asked Mean Mike if he had some whiskey, as the others had theirs stolen. He gave me his whiskey and I poured some on the old man's wound. Then I boiled up water and gathered what salt we had among us so that I could keep washing the injury with salted water to draw the infection out then and later during the night.

Finally, around the fire, Mean Mike confided what he had been up to for the three days he was gone from us. First, we told him the two stories that we had heard about him. When he heard the stories, he said that they were both right in a sense. He said that he had a reason to leave the morning after he came home drunk. He remembered that he was to meet the pretty little Chinese girl who had taken half of our gold for the rocker. Before he had gotten drunk, she had spoken to him at Fort Hope and asked him to meet her the next afternoon. He had imagined that she was madly in love with him, and maybe they would be off together for a while.

Yes, she could speak English, but had acted like she couldn't at Murderer's Bar. When Mike got to the fort, the pretty little Chinese girl was waiting for him with several Chinese men. She asked Mean Mike to come with them because they needed to talk to him, so he went with them to their camp along the river near Murderer's Bar.

Mean Mike said that he was excited. "I thought they wanted to discuss the girl and me getting married. I guess I am desperate for a wife after being stuck with ya varmints for weeks. It turned out the girl was married to one of the men with her. I felt as foolish as a sheep in a wolf pack. Long story short, the girl asked me to help them meet with a white man and Indian who wanted to buy firewater and guns from them. They had done business with the two men in the past. Their attitude had changed because of reports that the Indians were attacking all gold seekers, including any Chinese among them. Since then, they decided not to sell firewater and guns to the two now, they wanted me, as a white person of big size, to add authority to their answer of no deal with the men. The Chinese thought they might get threatened, but not so if I was with them."

Seph said to Mike, "Well, you do look like a bodyguard, but you were facing two against one if things got nasty. Did you stay or leave?"

"I wasn't too frightened, and the Chinese offered me a small pouch of opium for staying, and I wanted to try it to see if it is better than liquor. Before long, two men, one an Indian and one white, came into the Chinese camp. The white guy said, looking to the Chinese group, 'Who's this?' meaning me. The girl said, 'This is Mr. Mean Mike, he is our friend and our new partner. He took all our firewater and guns. So, sorry we have none for sale now.'

"The two, the white man and the Indian, looked at me and said, 'We'll do business with you then.'

"'Maybe,' I said. 'Meet me tonight at the saloon at the fort.'

"'We'll be there,' the white guy said, and then they left, and I collected my opium and left the Chinese camp."

Seph was more worldly than Jacque and me, and he said to Mean Mike, "Was the opium a brown powder substance?"

"It was," Mean Mike said. "I didn't know what to do with the opium, but I did not want to ask the Chinese. At the fort, I asked around, and I was told to smoke it. I went and bought a pipe because I just chew tobacco. Then I went to the saloon and sat a table with a glass of whiskey and drank it so fast that I went and bought another bottle of it. I laid it on the table with the intention of smoking opium and drinking. I found that I had a terrible thirst for the whiskey and finished half the bottle before taking up my pipe and opium powder. I put the powder in the bowl of my pipe and tried to light my pipe. After several tries, I got mad as I do, and threw the damn pipe across the room and it hit Frenchy who looked at me like I was in for another fight. Before he could get up from his table of friends and get to me, the white man and Indian entered the saloon and came to my table.

"Since I knew Frenchy would be on his way to see me, I invited the two men to sit down at the table with me. They were seating themselves when Frenchy came over and said to me, 'Get up and come outside. You must want another fight, or you wouldn't have thrown that pipe at me. This time I'm going break you of the habit of picking fights. Tonight, I'm not so drunk that I don't know what I'm doing. You asked for a lickin' and now you're goin' to get it.'

"'Wait a minute,' the white man said, 'We've got business with this guy first, so go sit down and wait your turn. You can still fight him when we're done talking to him. We won't be long.'

"'He started with me first, and by the time I'm done with him, he won't be able to talk, so sit there and shut up. Wait till I'm finished with him,' Frenchy snarled at the white man.

"'Gentlemen,' I said to the three men, 'Hear me out. Frenchy, I was frustrated with my pipe, and I threw it in anger. Here is the opium powder that I couldn't get to light in my pipe. Take the opium and smoke it because we both don't want to fight. Neither of us is drunk enough yet. Ya two fellows, the Chinese lied to ya; I don't have their firewater or guns. They used me to deceive ya,' I said to them.

"'Is it honest-to-God opium powder?' Frenchy asked, picking up the opium that I'd offered him. 'Shit! I've never seen the stuff before, but I've heard of opium dens,' Frenchy continued like a new friend.

"The white man and the Indian rose in anger from the table. 'To hell with this,' the white man yelled, 'You sons of bitches are working together, and we want in on the firewater and rifles. We want to buy the same amount as we have been buying from the Chinese.'

"Frenchy said in the white man's face, 'So what are you going to do to make us sell them to you?' The white man was fast and furious as he grabbed the opium from Frenchy's hand and threw it in the fireplace full of coals from supper. Then he punched Frenchy in the gut and face in two quick, mean jabs. The Indian pulled a knife and was about to stab Frenchy when I hit him with the whiskey bottle, which slowed him down enough for me to grab him. I shook him as I pulled him away from Frenchy. Frenchy recovered from his two jabs and smashed his fist in his opponent's gut, and he doubled over. I wrestled the knife away from the Indian and threw it in the coals of the fireplace. Both Frenchy and I had our opponents under control, and we dragged them to the door of the saloon and pushed them out.

"Then I offered Frenchy a drink at my table, and he accepted. We both admitted that the whole thing had been exciting. Quickly, we finished the part bottle of whiskey, and I bought another one. The strange thing was that the room seemed to have yellow smoke in it. There was nothing but the opium powder and the knife in the coals of the fireplace, but it was smoky. For a time, everything was feeling so damn good for both of us, like it never had been before and never would be again. Both of us were bruised up and sore from fighting the night before, but all our soreness, aches, bruises, and scraped skin felt whole and completely restored. Then we both felt so tired and lethargic that we stretched out on the floor by the fireplace and slept like babies.

"The bartender had tried to wake us several times, but we were sleeping so soundly that he could not rouse us. In his effort to get us awake, he too encountered the yellow smoke from the fireplace and got very sleepy himself. He might have fallen asleep too, but the two men wanting to buy firewater and guns came in with two helpers and dragged Frenchy and me outside the saloon. They poured water on us, and we slept through it. They decided they would throw us in the river, and we would either wake up or drown. Thankfully, Frenchy's friends, who included three of his brothers, came along and set us free from being dragged as sleeping captives into the Fraser.

"I awoke the next morning in the camp that was Frenchy's and his partners'. His partners were all French from France, not Quebec, and spoke French together. Frenchy was awake before me, and he could not remember too many details about what had happened to us. Frenchy and I shook hands and declared from then on, we would fight together, not against each other. Frenchy and his group went to Murderer's Bar to seek gold, and I headed back to the fort.

"About the other story about me and Frenchy joining a militia; at the fort, two men called themselves representatives of the magistrate at Fort Yale and were asking for volunteers to fight the Indians. They said that the magistrate at Yale named Captain Whannell, a former cavalry officer from Australia, was trying to form and lead a militia to fight the Indians. Frenchy and I were willing to help until we found that it was the gold hunters who wanted to create the militia at Yale to go out and attack the Indians. We also found out that the miners were willing to take the law into their own hands. They planned to attack Indian villages and kill as many natives as necessary to force the Indians into peace treaties. Frenchy and I wanted no part of attacking villages with women and children as the victims."

"Is there a reason for the Indian hostility against the gold seekers?" I asked Mean Mike.

"Ya bet," he said, but could not say more because Jacque noted that he heard Old Man Magee calling. So, we all went to check on him.

CHAPTER 16

Walking in Death's Footsteps

OLD MAN MAGEE was delirious with a high fever. I bathed his wound with salted water to help disinfect and draw the infection. I put a cold, wet cloth on his forehead to cool down his fever, but I felt that his wound was too infected, his temperature was too high, he was too old, and even too thin and frail to make it through the night. I thought to myself, he will die, and in truth, I gave up on him recovering.

Jacque said, "His wound is not as red as it was."

Mean Mike touched his forehead and said, "He's not as fevered as he was."

Seph said, "I think he may outlive us all; there is nothing old or frail about Magee as he is catching fish one after another."

Old Man Magee, opened his eyes and rasped, "Haven't you fellows anything better to do than gather around an old man like he's going to die? Nothing Brown has got the heart of a doctor, and an in with the Lord. I'm sure he'll get me through this." With that, he closed his eyes and went back to sleep.

It was as if a mule had kicked me between the eyes. Tears of shame wet my eyes, and I hung my head in guilt. I had no heart of a doctor.

I had given up on Old Man Magee, and I had forgotten about God. I knew God heals as doctors treat wounds and symptoms. I needed to trust God to heal and not give up hope in His help. It was time for me to apply what I knew about God in my life. Old Man Magee had more faith in God and me than I had.

Mean Mike looked at me and asked, "Ya okay, Nothing?"

"No," I said. "Maybe someday I'll have the heart of a doctor. Old Man Magee is counting on me and God to get him through this. I need to consult with God in prayer for an attitude adjustment in me."

"As ya want," Mean Mike said, and they all offered to sit with Old Man Magee during the night, but I said, "I want to honor his faith in God and me."

The others left, and I talked with God about Old Man Magee and what God thought about me becoming a doctor one day in the future.

In the morning Old Man Magee was improved, his fever had broken, the redness of the infection around his wound was less red, and he was hungry. It was apparent that his injury was healing, and he needed just to lie low and let it heal more.

As we worked the bar, Mean Mike answered my question about the need for a militia and the cause of Indian hostilities.

Mean Mike began, "We've seen it ourselves, the further we come up the Fraser River, the higher the number of people we find searching for gold. The natives see all these men invading their land. The intruders show the Indians little respect and are after their women for sex. The natives are at a disadvantage without as many guns. They also have collected some gold themselves and use it both to buy weapons and firewater. The whiskey makes them lose control and weakens them.

"A recent incident has the natives ready to kill those searching for gold. Two French gold seekers raped an Indian chief's daughter. In payback, the two Frenchmen were found floating headless in the Fraser. The Indians want to drive the miners from their land. They've been attacking them as they go beyond Yale to the Fraser Canyon and beyond. The miners at Fort Yale want to form a militia to attack the Indians and force them into peace treaties.

"Fort Yale is said to have two thousand or more people there, the majority of them gold hunters determined to push up the Fraser further and further to grab the gold. The British are moving to take more control over the miners and natives, but it is lawless and potentially deadly right now and will be for the foreseeable future."

"Where does that leave us?" I asked.

"We search for gold in the footsteps of greed and death. It makes me wonder if it is worth it. Who were the eight men we buried here? It cost them their lives. How many will get out alive, and how many will die here?" Jacque questioned.

"We'll get out alive if we have each other's backs, and Mean Mike doesn't go after a Chinese wife again," Seph answered.

CHAPTER 17
Innocence Lost

WE TOOK OUR time moving up the Fraser toward Fort Yale. I said that we were blessed, but the others said that we were lucky in our good fortune in finding gold. We learned that many miners were waiting at Fort Yale for a militia to break the danger from the Indians. They feared Indian attacks while looking for gold. We understood this since we had buried eight gold hunters killed by Indians. That act of concern for the dead bodies was turned against us.

Before we left the bar with the dead bodies, a group of miners came upon us. It was Frenchy and his brothers and other partners from Murderer's Bar. We were ready to move on and said the bar was all theirs to work if they wanted it. They were suspicious that we would abandon a bar when they came along. We explained it had nothing to do with them, that we had been there for a few days and felt it was time for us to keep moving on. We also said that we had found eight men there killed by Indians and that we had buried their bodies. We said we felt it was a sad and unlucky place.

Frenchy spoke English, as did Pierre his one brother, and the others spoke French, so Jacque could understand their conversations. They questioned among themselves who would waste time burying dead bodies. In their thinking, the bodies just needed to be thrown in the river, and it would carry them away. Maybe we killed the miners for their gold? Perhaps we had gold from eight miners? Would we come back to try and kill them? They decided that we had at least stripped the dead bodies of their valuables, and we did not want them to see any evidence of other watches, rings, pistols, etc. They saw us as capable of murder and theft. They intended to get us drinking and gambling to see if we had lots of gold among us. It seemed it was them who had a heart for theft and maybe murder.

We were not without our suspicions about them. They had in their company two females — one a young Indian girl, and the other a Chinese woman. They also had a young Indian brave, and all three seemed to be slaves against their will. We suspected the three had been stolen or bought. Jacque, as a fur trader, spoke native languages. He could also communicate with the two Indians with hand signs. It was quickly confirmed that the Indians were captives of the whites.

The French group suggested we stay with them at the camp we were vacating for some drinking and gambling. They proposed that for a small price we could have the companionship of either of the two females. Mean Mike was excited, insisting that maybe this time a Chinese woman would fall in love with him. Old Man Magee stunned everyone when he insisted that he wanted time with the Indian girl. He said, "If I die during sex, I will die happy." The French, including Frenchy, hooted, hollered, and smirked when Seph said, "I'll take the brave, I'm not proud."

Jacque said, "Let me drink your liquor with you while the others are busy. Our whiskey was stolen. Nothing Brown will prepare some beans and bacon and biscuits for a meal. Just let me get him started as he does not know what to do unless he is shown." Jacque spoke loudly that the bacon was packed in the canoe, so was the frying pan and pot packed near the middle of the boat. The beans were there along with the flour for the biscuits. As he directed me to the canoe and the supplies already packed, he whispered to me to do something to the food to make them sick. I nodded in reply.

Meanwhile, Mean Mike whisked the Chinese woman off among the trees, where he suggested that she hide or run off. He questioned her, "Aren't they keeping ya against ya will?"

"No," she explained, "I'm a prostitute. They have allowed me to work as one while traveling with them to Fort Yale, where I'll have a tent or house for my business. I'm very good at making men happy. They like me, and you will too." She then grabbed Mean Mike and started unbuttoning his shirt. It seemed that Pierre knew the Chinese lady was a fast worker for before Mike's shirt was entirely undone; they were interrupted.

"Lotus Blossom, where are you?" a male voice was whining.

"Stop it, Pierre," the Chinese woman yelled. "I'm a harlot, and I make all men happy, not just you. It is how I make a good living!"

"Don't make him happy, marry me instead. Just make me happy," whined Pierre. "Don't you love me? I love you!" Pierre added.

"Yes, I love you, Pierre, but I love all men," Lotus Blossom said.

"Well then, if you love all men, I'm going to shoot myself dead," Pierre yelled.

"Will he shoot himself?" Mean Mike asked.

"Maybe," the Chinese woman said, as if it didn't matter.

"But it sounds like he loves you," Mean Mike offered.

"He'll forget me, and I'll get rich at Fort Yale. It is not personal; it is just business. Thousands of lonely men are ahead of me at Yale, many with a little or much gold. Their gold will make me truly happy. Making men happy paid well in California, and it will pay better here for there is less competition and greater aloneness in this endless wilderness," Lotus Blossom said in total conviction.

There was a shot, and the French and Mean Mike and Lotus Blossom all headed towards the direction of the shooting. There was a second shot, and Mean Mike and Lotus Blossom found Pierre first. He had shot into the trunk of a nearby tree.

Seeing Mike and Lotus Blossom, Pierre grumbled at Lotus Blossom, "If I'd shot myself dead, you wouldn't have even cared a bit. I don't love you anymore."

"Good," said Lotus Blossom, "I have no time for jealous men in my life. You better be ready to share women like me in this gold rush."

Mean Mike kept moving closer to Pierre as Pierre talked with Lotus Blossom, and he was able to snatch Pierre's gun out of his hand before he did shoot himself or someone else. Men from his group took Pierre back to camp, and Mean Mike passed on Lotus Blossom's invitation to make him happy.

Seph and Old Man Magee were not after sex but to give the Indian girl and brave a chance to escape, because they were being held against their will. They had been captured from the same Indian village. The French had taken them as protection. They kept the two visible: the young brave worked panning gold with them, and the girl preparing meals in camp so that Indian raiding war parties would see the two Indians and be less ready to attack them. The two Indians had only been with the French a short time but were not confident they could find their way back to their village. They were told to sneak out of camp and travel upriver, and that we would help them when we came in our canoes. If we missed them, they were to keep going on along the river until they came to the next gravel bar, and we would find them there.

Mean Mike returned to camp, had a drink with the French, and offered to help me fix the meal. Old Man Magee returned, looking proud of himself and brought out his violin and set to playing lively tunes for the French group. Seph returned last and said the brave needed to recover a bit before returning to camp. I served up beans and bacon and biscuits to the French group and Lotus Blossom. The French did not seem to notice the absence of the two Indians. When they did, Mean Mike said we do not eat with Indians, but they can eat when we are done. The biscuits were safe as were the strips of bacon, but the beans were intended to upset the stomach and cause sickness.

To the beans, I had been extra generous with molasses. I had poured every bit of bacon grease into the beans so that they were as greasy as I could make them. The weed burdock was growing near the camp, and I cut two stocks of it as it looks like rhubarb. I cut the burdock stems into tiny pieces and added them to the bean pot. Burdock looks like rhubarb, but it isn't edible. I was praying I just added enough to make folks sick, not dead. I did not have much salt to add to the beans but emptied every bit of pepper we had in our supplies into them. When I tasted the beans, there was a strong molasses flavor, and I asked Mean Mike for some whiskey for the beans. I was hoping a little whiskey would help hide the burdock, pepper, and extra grease taste. It wasn't uncommon to have beans tasting like molasses.

The French were a little drunk and ate with a good appetite. We made an honest show of eating the biscuits and bacon and took helpings of beans, which we managed to leave on the ground or wherever we could hide them. Even though Mean Mike was warned not to eat the beans, he ate them like they were candies, and I worried I might have killed him.

When the meal ended, the French wanted to drink and gamble, but Seph said we needed to head on before it was too late in the day. The French said it was time to pay for the sex that the three of us had.

Mean Mike looked at Pierre and said, "I didn't have sex with Lotus Blossom, because of your yelling at us and your shooting."

Old Man Magee said, "Are you sure that Indian girl ain't got something? I am itchy as hell. Did you give me that girl on purpose to give me the itch? You must have it yourselves. I'm not paying you anything!"

Seph also cut in, accusing, "That Indian buck has open sores on his ass. What is wrong with him? He said you did it to him. I wasn't going near him. I'm not paying for disease!"

The Chinese lady started screaming at the French, "You better not have given me the itch or anything else. Why were you with them? You had me! You bastards! You didn't pay them, did you?"

The French were looking at each other in stress and guilt. There were accusations among themselves and denials. The stress and the bean pot contents erupted in either vomiting or running off with cramps. We looked at Mean Mike and were horrified at the thought of all the beans he had eaten, but then we remembered that he had his own canoe now. While the French were being ill or being called on for toilet duty, we left them to our old camp.

We did spot the Indian pair making their way along the shore of the river. There was room in Mike's canoe for them, but we were worried they would be okay riding in his canoe if Mike threw up or had cramps. To this day, none of us could believe the beans did not affect Mean Mike.

CHAPTER 18

Going Alone

AT THE NEXT bar, the first thing that needed to be done was to help get the Indian girl and brave back to their people. Old Man Magee and Seph made it clear to the rest of us that they had no sex with the girl and the brave; they just wanted to upset the French with their lies. Jacque was confident he could guide the girl and brave home, and it was decided they would travel downriver in Mean Mike's canoe. When the Indian pair had been first captured in the woods, they were taken to one bar before Murderer's Bar. If they got there, it would be a matter of going north inland from the river to locate their tribe. Jacque felt he knew where their tribe could be found for the pair confirmed that their tribe had traded their furs with Hudson's Bay fur traders. They set off the next morning, and Jacque insisted that he could go alone and that once in the woods, he and the Indians would be in a territory they could manage.

We felt Jacque should have one of us with him, but he refused any company. He thought that in the woods, Mean Mike was as quiet as a moose bellowing in mating season. Jacque also felt that I was too kind to fight to kill. He believed that Seph and Old Man Magee were needed in the gold searching. We all recognized that Old Man Magee was the master at keeping our camp. Seph was the steady hand that kept us rotating between panning and using the rocker. The bar we had arrived at had some Chinese working it and some other whites. Seph was needed there, for Mean Mike was more about fighting than sharing with others on any bar we worked. There was a space for us to work on the bar.

The white miners on the bar were friendly and talkative. They came with the names Belly Baggs, and his brother Freckled Baggs, Dad Bill, Popcorn Pete, and One-Foot-Charlie. Seph said they all should have been named talk-your-ear-off. They were kin and kind from the Blue Ridge Mountains of Tennessee. They had made a little money in the California Gold Rush and wanted a bit more before going home. These were married men with wives and kids waiting for them, and they sent their money from gold searching to their large families. They were on their way down the Fraser gathering gold on the bars as they went home towards Tennessee.

They were mountain men, but the farther they had gone up the Fraser, the more they decided the mountains in Canada were too high, vast, and mean to manage. They had already made their way well past Yale to Hells Gate, to Lytton, and even along the Thompson River for a short distance. They had been among the first on Hill's Bar, and they had struck gold there along with the others in good supply. We were not clear on where Lytton was or how the Fraser and Thomson River came together, but it seemed it would all be clear to us in time.

Unlike most gold seekers, they did not want all the gold they could get. They had found more than they hoped for and recognized they were in a wilderness that would not easily be tamed. They thought these Canadian mountains should be left to the Indians.

They informed us that miners at Fort Yale were split between a militia to go out to exterminate the Indians and a militia that would attack but also seek peace treaties with them. An army of 123 volunteers had left from Yale to show force towards the Indians. This army was under Captain Snyder, who wanted peace treaties. They did not know how it would turn out, but as we got nearer to Fort Yale, we would hear. The Indian threat might be resolved or be worse by the time we got there.

The gravel bar we shared with the mountain men was not large, but it was rich, and we spent a very profitable time there. The Chinese kept to themselves, but the mountain men loved to hear Old Man Magee on his fiddle, and when he sang, they listened spellbound. They had among them a fisherman or two and someone who hunted for their meat. They had shot a deer and had the carcass hung near their camp. After a day, they would butcher it and smoke most of the deer meat to preserve it. Some of it they would trade with other miners they met needing meat.

We had not considered the deer carcass to be dangerous until we heard a terrible roar from their camp in the night. A huge grizzly was frustrated with the deer carcass. He wanted to carry it off. The rope holding it to a tree limb would not let the grizzly carry it off in its mouth. The bear was up on its hind legs, growling and swatting at the rope holding the carcass, and the mountain men were frozen at the sight and sound of it. They were familiar with black bears but not the size and fury of the grizzly intent on eating their meat. We were hoping they would back off and leave the grizzly alone, for it was intent on the carcass, not them. In the moonlight, the bear seemed like a huge monster, and everyone in both camps had their guns ready to shoot at it. We were hoping it did not come to that, for a grizzly can have way more than nine lives.

Old Man Magee had been quietly adding kindling to the live coals of our campfire and had it burning brighter and brighter. Wild animals will shy away from open flames. He was hoping the mountain men might notice and build up their fire to keep the grizzly from coming into their camp. We thought, "Thank God!" when the grizzly began moving off with the deer carcass; it had shredded the rope holding the body to the tree limb. The mountain men wouldn't have the bear leave with their meat.

Dad Bill yelled, "We'll surround it. Shoot for the head or belly. Popcorn, you and Charlie put your lead in the hind legs."

Belly and Freckled Baggs and Dad Bill moved fast to surround the bear and sent their shots at the grizzly's head. The bear dropped the carcass and stood on its hind legs seeing the men surround it. The grizzly was roaring while swinging its front legs and paws, ready to take on all comers. No doubt the mountain men were good shots, but the bear's head was swaying from side to side, and their shots at its head caused it only anger, so it roared louder. The bear did not react to the shots at its hind legs.

Seph said that we better get over there and help, or we'll have bodies to bury again. Mean Mike ran over recklessly and jammed his rifle into the back of the bear and fired his rife. Faster than lightning, the bear turned its torso and swatted Mean Mike with his mighty paw, sending Mike and his rifle flying in the air. Seph was able to put a bullet in the nose of the grizzly, and it paused for a few seconds, and the three mountain men got shots into its head also. The grizzly crumpled to the ground. The mountain men set to work to skin it as they eagerly wanted the bear hide. They wanted the bear meat to smoke along with the deer carcass they had.

CHAPTER 19

A Bruise for a Bruise

THE BLOW THAT Mean Mike received from the bear did cause him some slight confusion. Thankfully, he didn't suffer from a severe concussion this time, for the bear's paw hit him in the chest, not the head. He had a huge purple bruise on his chest that was tender to touch. It didn't slow him down long. He took a day to rest up but then was ready to return to work on the bar.

The mountain men spent a day after the bear attack smoking their deer and bear meat. They would smoke it more at the next bar they stopped at on their way downriver. We did not speak to them or them to us. They were offended at us for helping in their fight with the bear. The night after the bear attack, Dad Bill, Belly, and Freckled Baggs passed around a jug of homemade drink amongst themselves. We had not realized Dad Bill was the father of Belly and Freckled Baggs since Dad Bill never used the last name for himself. Popcorn Pete was a third cousin and did not rate to share their hard cider mixed with berry juices and other secret ingredients.

One-Foot-Charlie was from the Tennessee Smokies and fell into partnership with the others, but he was not kin to any of them. Popcorn Pete had been a friend of Charlie's before Charlie had his foot shot off, the victim of a blood feud back at Leiper's Fork on the Natchez Trace Trail in Tennessee. Popcorn Pete doctored Charlie when his foot was chewed to pieces with the blast of the shotgun. Charlie was mistaken as one Eb Jones. The shooter shot Charlie's foot with a shotgun because Eb Jones had stolen a pair of boots from the shooter's kin. Folks in Tennessee, it seemed, had long memories, and refused to let any offense be forgotten.

Popcorn Pete did the doctoring in the community of Leiper's Fork. He wasn't a trained doctor; just a person folks went to when they were sick or injured. It was Popcorn Pete who amputated Charlie's foot and fitted the leg stump with a wooden shoe that was buckled on and off the stump. Popcorn Pete had a gift for doctoring, and the Baggs, his cousins, knew it. The Baggs were not much good at farming thin mountain soil, but they were good hunters. The more the people poured in to settle along the Natchez Trace, the more the game became scarce. The Baggs men left to go west to see where they might relocate their families and to send back whatever money they could until they could get back home again.

One-Foot-Charlie and Popcorn Pete came over to our camp the night after the bear attack. They said once the Baggs men got into their hard cider, they were in their own world, ending in a deep sleep that would hold till noon the next day. They said that Belly, Freckled, and Dad were good men in their own way. They had helped Popcorn Pete because he was their kin.

Popcorn had fallen into debt doctoring others, so that he had no money for taxes. Even after his cabin and everything he had was sold, he was still in debt. The Baggs paid his debt and said he could pay them back by traveling with them and working off the tax money they had paid for him. He agreed to it as long as One-Foot-Charlie could come along. Charlie was willing to work also. The Baggs stuck to trapping furs, and Popcorn and Charlie scraped hides working in their fur trade work.

When the price of furs was low, and the fur market was disappearing, they tried getting in on the gold rush in California. They made enough money in California to make them want to come to Canada. The Baggs had a vast proud streak about their ability to hunt and kill any animal. With Mean Mike and Seph joining in their fight with the bear, they could not claim they killed the grizzly by themselves. They could not forgive Seph and Mean Mike for interfering so they would move on from the bar the next day.

I asked, "How long will they refuse to forgive Mike and Seph?"

Popcorn Pete said, "They won't forgive what Mike and Seph did ever, as there is no way to make it right. Because Mike and Seph acted with concern for their success and safety in killing the bear, they'll not seek an act of revenge on them."

One-Foot-Charlie explained that the Baggs do not read or write. Their learning is about doing what they need to do in work, hunting, and providing for their family. They have been taught to memorize a few Bible passages that give them their code for life. Their lives are: "A life for a life, an eye for an eye, a foot for a foot, a burn for a burn, a wound for a wound, a bruise for a bruise." Many folks take something from the Bible to explain why they do what they do.

I could not disagree with One-Foot's belief that people like to blame their behavior on the Good Book. "Do the Baggs have any teachings from Jesus memorized?" I asked.

"They do not hold with Jesus and the New Testament much. They say if you forgive, help, heal, feed the multitudes, you'll still get crucified. Forgiveness and mercy don't work but getting even with others does. They feel that people respect a life for a life," Popcorn Pete answered.

One-Foot-Charlie offered that the Baggs come honestly to right or wrong thinking. In Tennessee, you have to decide between the North and the South. Folks there are ready to argue and fight for their side. You are either for slavery or against it. Slavery is either right or wrong. People are prepared to take the side of what they see as right and fight those that they see as wrong.

Popcorn Pete asked, "You ever read a book called *Uncle's Tom's Cabin?*"

Seph, Old Man Magee, and I had read the book.

"It's held in great regard in the North and rejected in the South," Popcorn Pete said. "The plantation economy of the South is based on slavery and the white supremacy of landowners who see the colored slaves like livestock, mere beasts to work, use, or sell. When we return across the border, the Baggs are ready to head back East or to Texas, for the South will soon leave the union, and the North and South will fight it out. The Baggs are for the South. Charlie and I are for the North. I have always wanted to be trained as a doctor and surgeon. In a war, the wounded are at the mercy of a doctor. I have no heart for fighting and killing, but I do want to gain skill at doctoring and healing. I have no desire to own another person, whatever their color."

One-Foot-Charlie said, "Here all that matters is finding gold. It is wild, untamed land administered through the Hudson's Bay Fur Trading Company forts and a handful of British officials busy claiming this wilderness for the British Empire. They want their share of the gold for keeping law and order. Many are coming in for the gold rush, but how many will stay when the gold rush is over? Tall, wild mountains are not easy to settle."

Popcorn Pete said, "The difference is that in America, the people of the East will move West and claim any wilderness they find for themselves. The Indians that live in the wilderness are considered savages that cannot be trusted. Whatever lies between the Mexican border and the Canadian border is to become land for settlement. The American way is about fighting. We fought to get rid of the British. We have fought against Mexico and Canada and will likely do so again. We have and will continue to fight the Indians, and we will fight each other over having slavery or not having slavery. We want to keep living by the sword and dying by the sword."

Seph spoke up. "You're saying that we Americans demand that it is our way or no way and kill others to have it our way. We don't kill others because we disagree with them. We only kill for a good reason, like to protect ourselves. Those who want to fight for slavery or against it will go East or to Texas to fight in that war if it happens."

"If Abraham Lincoln wins the election next year, people will be killing each other over slavery. You better start thinking about which side that you'll fight on when you go home to America. In war, even those who don't take a side still get killed," Popcorn Pete said to Seph.

"The war won't come to the Pacific Coast. It won't matter in California or Oregon or Washington Territories," Seph stated.

"I hope you are right," Popcorn Pete replied.

One-Foot-Charlie said, "But in the Oregon and Washington Territories there are ongoing battles with the Paiute, Shoshone, and Bannock tribes which also turn into recurring wars and will continue to do so until the Indians are killed or forced to reservations. Will we ever quit fighting and killing?" Not waiting for comments, One-Foot-Charlie announced he was heading back to their camp as packing up and moving the next day would be lots of work. Popcorn Pete said that he would be coming back to their camp soon.

I was bold and asked Popcorn Pete if he had some gold set aside so he could train as a doctor. He said that he had a little, but he and Charlie only got whatever gold they found one day a week. Six days out of seven, any gold they found went to the Baggs. The Baggs were okay with him and Charlie staying at the coast in Canada when they finished going down the Fraser. To the Baggs, Popcorn Pete was a-weak-kin because his heart wasn't really into hunting and fighting. His desire to help sick and hurting people, even Indians and enemies, was embarrassing and honestly, he lacked common sense. Living in

Canada under British rule was insulting to the mountain men. The gold they found in Canada was good, but nothing else was.

Seph offered that most Americans would likely return home. Some would end up staying after the gold rush as the land opened up with the building of roads and settlements developed. Popcorn Pete said that was what he was counting on and bid us a good night to return to his camp.

Popcorn Pete had only been gone a short while when shots rang out from their camp. We grabbed our guns and hightailed it over. The Baggs, Belly, Freckled, and Dad Bill were firing their rifles in the air, celebrating something induced by their drinking. We did not stick around, knowing they might take a shot or two at us. The next day they broke camp, loaded their supplies, and headed down the Fraser. One-Foot-Charlie and Popcorn Pete waved a farewell to us, but the Baggs ignored us.

CHAPTER 20
Going, Coming, and Going Again

WE WERE MARKING time waiting for Jacque to return, reluctant to move further up the Fraser, so we began to pan for gold and use the rocker on the bar we had been at for some days. We had found a good amount of gold, and our attitude was that there was no more to be found. The mountain men had moved on, and the Chinese, so it seemed strange to work on the bar alone. Old Man Magee was the first to find a small gold nugget, not just tiny particles of gold. Mean Mike was next and then Seph and then me. We were giddy with excitement and joy. The bar had been kind to us but was spoiling us with an unexpected abundance. We were focused on finding gold when we heard a sharp whistle. It was Jacque's whistle, and he was coming towards us in Mean Mike's canoe as fast as he could paddle. Were two boats chasing him?

We dropped our shovels and gold pans, left the bar, and got our rifles ready to protect Jacque as he came closer in his canoe. No protection was needed, because the two canoes, filled with three Indians in each, were accompanying Jacque to see him safely back to us. They were very thankful for the return of the Indian girl and the brave. Strange coincidence, Jacque had a carcass of deer he had killed recently. A deer carcass was still fresh in our minds. Jacque had brought it for our food. We, of course, roasted the meat and shared it with the Indians who had come with Jacque to our camp. These Indians understood returning one good deed for another in seeing Jacque returned to us safely. They were also aware that the gold the white men like us sought along the river, was valuable to us like furs. The Indians had hoped to find the shiny particles themselves and use it buy goods at the forts. They were slow to take an interest in gold, and now they were treated as if they had no right to it at all.

I felt it wasn't fair, and we talked together about the cheating of the Indians in the gold search. We had found more than our share of gold on the bar. That morning alone, we had discovered more than six nuggets of gold. I suggested we give each Indian a gold nugget. These nuggets were a bit bigger, and whites could not claim them worthless to cheat the Indians when they went to trade them for goods. The others agreed with me, and we gave the gold to them after they had eaten with us. Old Man Magee played his violin, but the Indians knew of it as a white man's fiddle. They liked his music. The two Indian canoes left down the Fraser with respect in their hearts toward us and we toward them.

It was good to have Jacque back with us again for we counted on each other and knew we were stronger together than apart. Each person strengthened the rest, we were closer than brothers and more than friends. In this wilderness of nature and men, we were family. We told Jacque about the mountain men, Belly, Freckled, and Dad Bill who were angry at us for helping them kill a grizzly. He said that the grizzly skin or hide is very sought after by the Indians, and it could cause some of them to steal it or take it by force. We were sure the mountain men could hold their own, but Jacque wasn't as sure, as we were.

Jacque informed us that the Indians that were with him could not give him much information about the Indians ahead, especially after Fort Yale. Their chief was old and not excited to lead his tribe into battle against the whites along the river. Other chiefs had decided it was time to stop the whites and were ready to make war on them. We would probably encounter more of them as we continued to Fort Yale and beyond.

Once the Indians left, we continued to look for gold on the bar, for the days were growing much shorter and wetter. If the bar continued to amaze us with nuggets, we would not move on from our good fortune.

It was a day of visitors. Around dark, a canoe reached the bar and our camp. It contained one man we knew and one man we didn't. The man we knew was John Russ; the American sent back to America at his trial at Fort Langley. The man with Russ had the critical eye of a thief; he was interested in everything he could see and what he could not see. John Russ recognized us as friends of Judge Begbie and remembered us as no-good Indian lovers.

Russ said, "I never would've come near if I knew it was you bastards. Have they sent that jackass judge back to England?"

Mean Mike was quick to say, "We hear the judge is second to the governor now and making the Indians here British citizens!"

"That's bullshit," Russ snapped.

"Well, what can you expect from bastards?" Mean Mike offered. "By the way, watch ya-selves as ya continue up the river. Some of the Indians are taking revenge on the whites who molest and rape their women. They have cut heads off, but only after they've sliced off the whites' privates."

Russ was momentarily at a loss for words, and Jacque spoke up, "We would invite to warm yourself by our fire and to have a cup of tea, but I make the tea, and you don't like half-breeds like me, so maybe you should move on."

"You going to make me, breed?" Russ snarled.

"I might encourage you with this shotgun pointed at you," Old Man Magee said, adding, "I wouldn't wait too long, as I have an itchy finger and no aversion to spilled blood."

Russ and his companion paddled their canoe off into the night, but we could feel Russ's hate and desire to kill us if he could. Hate has an insatiable appetite. We knew we would need to keep night guards, for Russ and his friend might return to harm us, especially in the dark.

The next morning was like too many fall days that came our way; it was rainy and raw. The pouring rain complicated the search for gold, and we were soaked to the bone. Every time we thought we could not continue our work, the rain would let up, and by dark, we had more nuggets to show for our struggle. We tripled the six nuggets we had given to the Indians.

CHAPTER 21

Who Do You Believe?

WE CONTINUED SEARCHING on the gravel bar longer, for it continued to provide us with gold that thousands of others were eager to find. We were humbled at our good fortune but began to realize that our time for finding gold was near an end. Day by day, fall moved towards winter, and the cold, rain, sleet, and touches of snow dogged our existence. Some might search for gold no matter the season or weather, but it was not in us. We talked of spending the late fall and winter at Yale or New Westminster. Lady luck had been guiding and filling our gold pans, but we all knew spending the winter at Yale would eat up a great deal of the prosperity we had found with everything so expensive there. Mean Mike might work as a blacksmith, Seph as a bartender, and Jacque at the Hudson's Bay fort, but what would Old Man Magee and I do during the winter?

The other thing that we pondered was whether we would continue to search for gold together in the spring as we did now. We had succeeded as a group and trusted each other with our lives. Each of us struggled with the question, Where, do I go from here?" We all had made enough in this gold rush to take our wealth and go our own ways. I could begin some schooling to become a doctor at home in America or here in British Columbia if any training opportunities were possible. Old Man Magee could now find Mae as a man of some means rather than as a penniless drunk. Mean Mike thought of opening his own blacksmith business. Seph was considering running his own saloon. Jacque was thinking of guiding miners through the mountain passes used by the Hudson's Bay traders or returning to Oregon. Each of us worked on searching for gold, thankful we had positive options ahead of us. Many others were broke and hungry. Many drank, gambled, tried opium, fought, stole, and sank into despair at the knowledge whatever money they had was disappearing fast. Many left Yale for the coast in defeat but were replaced with even more arrivals eager to find gold.

Visitors found us as we were not more than three miles from Hill's Bar, and Fort Yale was close to it. We sent Jacque and Mean Mike to Yale to the assayer's office to exchange our gold for money. We needed a couple of sheets of canvas. One sheet was to cover fire-wood in the frequent rain, and another sheet to be stretched over tall poles to keep the rain off the campfire. We wanted another tent to have one more dry space for our sanity in the rain and mud. Supplies at Yale were expensive, and the place was full of temptation and trouble. Jacque and Mike did not linger there for a criminal element tended to follow those who came and went from the assayer's office.

Two chaplains from the Hudson's Bay Company, Ed and Burt with similar last names traveled with Mean Mike and Jacque from Hill's Bar. As Mike and Jacque passed Hill's Bar, the two chaplains were canoeing on their way to Fort Hope. It was another cold and wet day, and they welcomed the chance to share our campfire, which we were able to put under a canvas roof thanks to Jacque and Mike. With the days growing shorter in daylight, we were ready to visit with the two men in the long evening. Although the chaplains worked mainly with the Hudson's Bay officials, employees, and their families, they also ministered to the gold seekers who occasionally sought spiritual help.

Ed had been serving longest and had found the gold prospectors mainly indifferent to God's word. He considered them opportunists willing to endure hunger, hardship, and failure with a deep conviction that tomorrow they would become rich. Too many of the miners were set on self-gratification, such as fighting, drinking, gambling, and womanizing.

Burt shared that he found the miners at Yale reckless, lawless, and full to overflowing in profanity. They had little recognition of the Sabbath or any pangs of conscience regarding prostitution. They harbored no honor or respect for any native women or the natives generally. He felt that it was no wonder war between the miners and the natives broke out during the summer. He told us of the summer war between the miners from Yale and the Indian tribes living in the Fraser Canyon. We had heard several things, but it was good to listen to the full story.

Burt felt that the natives took up arms to defend themselves from the relentless invasion of foreigners who were a law unto themselves. The aliens mined along the Fraser without permission from the Indian tribes. They prevented the natives from mining for gold themselves. When challenged by natives, the miners threatened them with violence. In seeking their gold, the miners disrupted the natives' salmon fishing in the Fraser Canyon. The miners occupied fishing areas and ruined critical spawning sites with mining sluices.

The miners at Yale formed a military company to take revenge on the Indians for the French men's deaths. Departing from Yale, they marched upriver to fight the natives. They were gone upriver about eight days, killing thirty-six natives, including five chiefs, and wounding many others. As the militia of miners came downriver, they burned five Indian villages to the ground and reportedly killed every man, woman, and child. They rescued about five miners from a group of twenty or twenty-five miners who were killed by Indians while searching for gold. Their attack on the natives only intensified the miners' resolve to use force to protect themselves from future Indian attacks. Some were advocating the need for miner militias to kill every native they saw.

A large group of miners of several hundred men left Yale about the middle of August under Captain Henry Snyder, who advocated reaching peace treaties with the natives rather than exterminating them. They set out for Kumsheen, where the Fraser and Thompson rivers meet. There Snyder met with Chief David Spintlum and eleven other chiefs and told them that they would confront more and more miner militias if they didn't get access to their goldfields. Chief Spintlum asked what the miners would do. The answer was that all the old people were going to be killed off, and only the young women would be kept.

One Indian chief told Snyder and the whites to stop their talk of killing right there. He offered the miners land. He indicated that the sunrise side of the river would belong to the whites, and the sunset side will belong to the natives. He told the whites that they were not to kill any of the native people. The whites agreed and put down their guns and shook hands with the Indian people. Peace was established on August 22 there at Kumsheen, and Snyder urged the native communities throughout the Fraser Canyon to fly white flags as a sign of peace. In late August, Governor James Douglas reached the Fraser Canyon to show that it was under British control, but the war between miners and Indians was over.

The peace established between the Indians and miners in August was still a reality in October as we talked about it around our campfire. Rather than have inevitable bloodshed, the native chiefs protected their people from miners who had no reluctance to kill those who got in the way of their lust for gold. The chaplains understood that the wilderness which had been mainly peaceful between the Indians and the limited white traders and trappers was gone. As employees of the Hudson's Bay Company, the Indians had been their traders and trappers, partners and friends, but now the natives were victims in their own lands. The chaplains were praying that the gold rush would turn out to be short-lived and that the invasion of miners would disappear as quickly as it began. They were not sure that the peace would last.

I reminded the chaplains of the lion and the lamb as a symbol of peace. I said that the predator and its potential victim could coexist in harmony. Anyone can fight and hate, but few seek to be peacemakers. People must want peace, not war. My Quaker roots of nonviolence shook my tongue loose with the words of Isaiah, "The wolf will live with the lamb, the leopard will lie down with the goat, the calf and the lion and the yearling together; and a little child will lead them. They will neither harm nor destroy on all my holy mountain." My words led to a lengthy discussion of predators in animals and among people. Can there be a world where there is neither harm nor destruction? Isn't there a difference between intentional harming or destroying and unintentional harming or killing?

Mean Mike asked the chaplains if harming and destroying didn't need to be avenged. "Shouldn't we take a life for a life, an eye for an eye, a tooth for a tooth, right down to a burn for a burn, and a bruise for a bruise?"

Chaplain Burt said that getting even is not the way of Jesus who taught; "Do not resist an evil person. If someone strikes you on the right cheek, turn to him the other also. And if someone wants to sue you and take your tunic, let him have your cloak as well." The chaplain finished with the instruction of Jesus. "Love your enemies and pray for those who persecute you."

Mean Mike and Seph seriously questioned if Jesus said to love your enemies, for they thought it was, love your neighbor and hate your enemies.

Old Man Magee said that some neighbors are harder to love than an enemy. We asked if he was talking about one of us, and he said, "Maybe," with a huge grin.

After much discussion, the chaplains concluded that we all had a long way to go before we would have the full knowledge of the Lord in heaven. The chaplains left in the morning, pleased to have had an evening of sharing and talking with us, and we with them.

CHAPTER 22

Known by our Reputation

BY THE FIRST week of November, we had reached our point of action. The five of us went to Yale to decide if or how we might stay there for the winter. We could add our two tents to the endless tents at Yale. The tents would keep the snow and rain off us, but they wouldn't be much buffer for the winter cold and icy winds. On the street beside the river, the shacks were built of wood boasting a generous number of saloons and houses of prostitution. The Hudson's Bay fort and store were made of wood along with a few other businesses, and it was rumored that the town would be surveyed next year, for actual streets and building lots.

There were a vast number of miners at Yale, many with too much time to discuss everything and nothing: they named every bar that gold was found on, they could tell you who had made it rich, and who was connected to the Hudson's Bay fort. They could identify the British officials there, the arrival and departure of the steamers, the danger of Indians, the best gambling places, the opium den in the Chinese area, the crooks, and the dangerous individuals and gangs. Among this large gathering of strangers, there was a massive circulation of common knowledge. We found this public opinion or common knowledge full of a dangerous mixture of lies and truth.

As the five of us explored Yale together, considering how it might fit into our winter plans, we found that we were the focus of many stares and with most miners giving us lots of space like we had a contagious disease or were dangerous to be near. We had barely started our tour of Yale when a man with a whole herd of miners behind him confronted us. He introduced himself as the constable of Yale and said that he wanted to know our identity and purpose at Yale.

Mean Mike spoke quickly with belligerence. "Is it a crime to walk into ya town? Have ya or someone else got something against one of us or all of us?"

"You five fit the description of a group called the Deadly Five. The Deadly Five are described as two giant men, one young and the other older, an old man, a small young man, and a breed," the constable answered.

"What have these Deadly Five been accused of doing?" Mean Mike belligerently asked again.

"It's rumored that the five killed eight miners on a bar for their gold and buried their bodies in one big grave," the constable answered.

"We came upon eight miners killed by Indians, and we buried them rather than leave their bodies to float away in the river. The Indians took the personal possessions or gold they had. What else do you claim we've done?"

"There's a story that the young giant sells guns and firewater to the Indians. That description fits you," the constable stated.

"That's a lie because if I had liquor, I'd drink it. I have my own gun and no more," Mean Mike said honestly.

"What other stories have you heard about us, constable?" Old Man Magee asked.

"It is said that the old man in the group is trigger happy with a shotgun and likes the color of whiskey and blood," the constable replied.

"There was a day I would have sold my blood for liquor, but now this old finger is pretty shaky and the shotgun none too steady. You can see with your own eyes I'm not much to be afraid of," Old Man Magee said with such conviction that everyone seemed to believe him.

"You have three left, constable. What have we done that is so deadly?" I asked.

"You, the small young one, are reported to put poison in peoples' food, the big older giant is called a sodomizer, and the breed a ghost ready to materialize when needed by the other four. It is said that the five of you are deadly for if one of you is crossed the others come to his aid," the constable offered.

Seph asked, "Do you have any evidence to back up these stories about us being the Deadly Five?"

"No," the constable added, "but you have lots of people concerned with seeing you in person. Whether it is true or not, many are going to regard you as the Deadly Five and avoid you."

"That's fine," Mean Mike said, "just keep us straight. I'm Mean Mike," and pointing to us he said, "This is Nothing Brown, Old Man Magee, Seph the Sodomizer, and Jacque the Ghost. I can blacksmith, Old Man Magee plays the fiddle and sings, Nothing Brown is a doctor in the making, and Seph is a first-class bartender. What town can ever have too many of such capable fellows? Last of all, the breed is our guardian angel and our true brother. He is an excellent guide to anyone who needs led through the wilderness."

The questions and answers might have continued, but the whistle of the steamer coming into dock distracted the crowd, and the constable came to us and said that Judge Begbie had been asking about us and was scheduled to hold court in Yale in a few days. When asked if the constable believed that we were the Deadly Five, he said that we were suspects until proven innocent. It wasn't what we wanted to hear.

We started to check out Front Street for Mean Mike, and Seph wanted to have a drink or two of liquor, but a second group of men met us. An aggressive man as their leader declared that they were the vigilante group at Yale. The constable was an agent of the British Crown and could not be trusted to look after the American miners at Yale. They intended to make sure the murderers of miners were not tolerated there.

Mean Mike said, "I can understand that. I invite ya to come out and tell me that ya know that I am a murderer of miners. Let us settle this man to man, or are ya a coward?"

"It wouldn't be a fair fight because of your size," the vigilante leader answered.

"Judging people on hearsay ain't fair either. Ya is a coward without any lick of justice to ya," Mike answered. "If ya weren't a coward, ya would come out and call me a murderer to my face," he challenged again.

"You've been warned. We're watching your gang and are ready to act," the vigilante said without much steam.

"Are ya ready to act, just like ya is ready to come out to face me? Ya is a coward, and ya whole group is a bunch of cowards," Mike said.

I'm not sure if Mean Mike was expecting to fight the whole group of eight vigilantes, but they came as a group to fight him. Seph jumped in beside Mean Mike, followed by Jacque and Old Man Magee. I let out my crazy shriek and ran at the advancing vigilantes who stopped to stare at my flopping and spinning around on the ground. Mean Mike picked up my shriek and began to run at the group who were in total shock. Mean Mike started to punch, and Seph began the shrieking also and hitting, and the vigilantes took off as if they had encountered a pack of wolves or devils. We were surprised to see that there had been a sizeable amount of people watching us. After the fight, people were convinced that we were a deadly five and would have nothing to do with us. One of the spectators had been Judge Begbie, and another was the constable of Yale.

Judge Begbie did not react to us like the others and greeted us like old friends. He was pleased to see the rehabilitation of Old Man Magee, who was sober and was glad that we had success searching for gold. He invited us to buy him dinner, which we did. The constable was not impressed with our friendship with the judge, and made it clear to us that we weren't welcome at Yale for the winter. He was convinced that we were mad dogs capable of anything. We would have to make other plans for ourselves for the winter.

CHAPTER 23
Heading Back to the Coast

JACQUE HAD FELT it before, but it was new to the rest of us. Miners at Yale treated us with mistrust, distaste, fear, and loathing. We were the entertainment for bored men unable to freely search for gold because of the weather. It was a welcome diversion to keep us as the center of their attention and hatred. It is said men have trouble showing love but have no problem with despising others that they see as wrong or criminal. The gold seekers considered us a deadly fivesome who had killed eight miners and were capable of every low-down crime they could imagine. Their only evidence was gossip, but it was more than enough for them to hate us. Our dispatch of the vigilantes only made them talk of the need for others to lynch us. The general talk was that it sure needed to be done by others.

We were shocked and unnerved, but quickly certain that Yale was not going to be our winter home. It was back to our camp and then decide what our trip to the coast would be. It would be easier to take a steamer to New Westminster, but that meant leaving our two canoes, two tents, rocker, gold pans, and various other gold mining equipment for others to take. We could not sell them at Yale, but Jacque said maybe we could find buyers at Hill's Bar.

117

If we were to go gold searching in the spring, we would need our existing equipment or new stuff then. It seemed then some of us would continue searching for gold, at least Mean Mike and Seph. Jacque was a probable, me a maybe, and Old Man Magee a not likely. We had tried to get the price of a steamer passage to the coast at Yale, but no one at the steamship office would deal with us, even for some information.

We decided that we should keep our equipment for whoever wanted it in the spring. Jacque was certain the Indian tribe to which we returned the young girl and brave would keep our supplies for us. They would be glad to use our canoes while we were away if they needed them. The tribe's location was on our way to Fort Hope, where we could catch a steamer going downriver to Fort Langley and New Westminster.

We would all go to the Indian village so they would know us individually if Jacque wasn't with us when we came for our equipment in the spring. We set the eleventh day of April to be at Fort Hope to look for gold as a group again. Jacque suggested that we hunt and bring food to the tribe for a special meal with them. He suggested we would need a least three deer for them.

We packed up our camp and headed towards Fort Hope. We decided to wait until we were closer to the Indian village to hunt for food to take to the tribe.

As we canoed downstream, we came to a small inlet filled with bulrushes and small willow trees. There, bigger than life, was a huge male moose feeding on willow leaves and paying us no never mind. Jacque was quick to tell us that a moose would feed a whole tribe. The rest of us were not too eager to take on a moose that seemed much bigger than the grizzly bear that took the mountain men and ourselves to kill. The wrack of antlers on the moose's head seemed bigger than me.

"How big is that thing?" I asked.

"A moose stands about six and a half feet tall, and that one will weigh about a thousand pounds," Jacque answered. "He will not lay down and die for us. We'll land at the edge of the inlet and go through the forest and come near the moose unseen. Then I'll try a mating call, and if he comes toward us, it will take everyone's shot to bring him down," he instructed us.

It was one of those times when Mean Mike, Seph, and I looked at each other with a mixture of excitement, and a missing backbone. A colossal moose seemed as likely to win a fight, as we would. Jacque was the only one confident among us about the outcome. Jacque insisted that Mean Mike walk quieter than he ever had before in the woods. Mike was to stay well behind us and barely able to see us. Mike was naturally clumsy and could make a lot of noise when he was trying to be quiet. Jacque explained that he hadn't practiced his moose calls since last fall. He felt that it might take a while to get his calling attractive to the moose. He would do his calls, and if the moose responded, we would hear the moose coming through the trees.

We pulled up at the edge of the inlet, and Old Man Magee was left to stay with the two canoes. We gathered up and loaded our guns and took extra ammunition. The three of us set off with Mean Mike behind us. Jacque had told us that we should not fire until the moose was about twenty feet away and take time to make sure we hit the moose in the head or shoulders, as misses would mean the moose would mate us. I could not see how Jacque could joke at such a time, and Seph looked like he wished he was anywhere else in the world but here.

Jacque snuck up to the inlet and reported we were straight north of the moose, still snacking on willow leaves. Jacque cupped his hands over his mouth and let out a sound that was supposed to imitate a female moose in heat. He tried several times, and I looked back at Mean Mike behind us on the trail who was mockingly using his hands each time Jacque made a call. When we had given up that the fake mating calls were going to work, there was the sound of crashing through the trees. With incredible speed, the moose was coming towards us with a great passion on his mind.

Jacque was the first to fire his rifle. Seph and I were in shock but got our wits about us, and we also shot at the moose. The three shots hit the moose, but they did not slow him down. Jacque fired again, and we fired a second time. The moose did veer and head in Mean Mike's direction. Mean Mike could not be seen, but another male moose came charging at the one we had shot. The two moose locked antlers, and the one already wounded by us was driven backward and down to the ground. Mean Mike appeared and shot the moose in the head, which was winning the battle between the two beasts. We raced up and shot the second moose also. Both moose died from our bullets. We were shaking and thankful to have two moose to give the natives. None of us were gloating over the two magnificent animals that we had killed. Their meat would provide food, but we all knew their lives were as valuable as our own in the wilderness.

The second moose that had appeared wasn't quite as big as the first moose, but both animals would supply vast quantities of meat. The meat would be more than we could transport to the Indian village, so some of the natives would need to come and help carry the meat to the village. Jacque went to bring villagers to help move the meat.

That left Seph, Mean Mike, and me to butcher the two moose. We wanted Old Man Magee to set up camp where we had anchored the canoes. He prepared our tents and cooked some food. We skinned one moose, then the next. We had to sever the heads with their racks of antlers. After gutting the beasts, we had to half, then quarter the carcasses. It was a hard job that had the two giants, Mike and Seph spent as we stored the meat at the camp Old Man Magee had set up for us. He realized we would need several fires burning during the night to help keep wolves and other hungry animals away from the meat. We would need guards during the night and the fires burning brightly. We were not sure what we would do if it rained and we could not count on the protection of the campfires.

I helped gather as much wood as could be found to feed the fires. When we stopped for supper, it was dark, and we were each bone tired. We, of course, had to talk about the grizzly bear that came after the mountain men's deer carcass. If a grizzly came to our camp, we sure would welcome all the help the mountain men might give us, not resent it. We harbored no great pride in our ability to kill bears or moose. The skins of the moose would provide material for making moccasins and clothing for the Indians. We had no idea if the natives used the heads or antlers. We felt good about being able to give the tribe food.

We were thankful that it did not rain that night or the next day as we waited for Jacque to come with Indians to transport the moose meat. On the third day, Jacque returned by himself. He had been unable to find the Indian tribe as they had moved to a different area for the coming winter season. We were closer to Hill's Bar than Fort Hope, so we would take the meat there to sell it. We did not want it wasted. We left our camp set up and filled the canoes with the moose meat. Jacque guided our first boat with me and old Man Magee helping with the paddling. Mean Mike and Seph followed us in the second canoe. Many of the people at Hill's Bar were going to winter there rather than at Yale. We did not know there had been a history of friction between the Hill and Yale. We were able to sell the moose meat and split the money between us. We returned to our camp by dark and set our plans to go on to Fort Hope.

We hoped maybe we could find a friend of Jacque with the Hudson's Bay fort who might keep for us our canoes and gold mining equipment until the spring. We agreed that we would give the person the money we had made from the sale of moose meat

121

to encourage the person's willingness. It was a significant sum of money. Food and meat were costly and limited in supply for the gold seekers. Our canoeing to Hope was uneventful.

At Hope, Jacque found an employee at the Hudson's Bay fort that was willing to keep and protect our equipment during the winter. The employee was very thrilled with the money offered to him. With our canoes and equipment stored, we felt naked. We were all down to the clothes on our backs and a backpack of personal possessions. We all felt homeless, as if the tent and camps we shared, and even our canoes, gave us an identity and security. Some miners go mad in the wilderness from loneliness and isolation. The five of us scattered the power of wilderness that could close about you like a prison.

As we made our way on the steamer, we were no longer thinking and acting like one. Mean Mike and Seph quickly went to drink some welcome liquor. Old Man Magee had splurged for a little cabin on the steamer. There he could shave and bathe as he was intent on cleaning up for his coming meeting with Mae. He genuinely seemed to need time to rest and gather himself. The thought of becoming a sober husband was intimidating him.

Jacque had learned that the pilot on the steamer was someone that he knew. Jacque was helping him with the measuring of water levels in the river. Like the pilot, Jacque could read by sight the river current and its force. It turned out that Jacque was related to the pilot and was busy working with him. I sensed that we who were known as the fearsome Deadly Five had splintered apart in a few minutes on the steamer.

CHAPTER 24
Medical Advice

I WAS ALARMED to hear there had been a fight with knives on the steamer, and one man was dead, another cut up badly. All I could think of was that maybe it involved Mean Mike. I rushed to the area of the fight to find in pure relief that neither the dead man nor the cut and bleeding man was Mike. A middle-aged man, a doctor it seemed, was trying to stop the severe knife wounds from bleeding profusely. He was making little headway on stitching up the cuts. I told the man I had worked with a doctor and would do whatever he needed doing.

He immediately had me holding cloths with pressure on the deep cuts to help stop the heavy bleeding. He brought out from his bag a reddish liquid, which he put on the cuts that he felt did not need stitches. He had me stitch a cut on the man's left forearm while he stitched a deep wound on his chest. When the cuts were stitched, he applied the reddish liquid, which he called iodine, to keep the cuts from getting infected. I told him that I had heard of cleansing wounds with salted water and using it on infected wounds, but I hadn't seen this iodine stuff before. He assured me that there were now more things that doctors could use to help people.

It turned out the doctor was a Dr. James Smith, a British physician who had begun his career as an apothecary. He did his mandatory half a year apprenticeship in a London hospital. He could have studied at an infirmary or dispensary as well. At the hospital, the surgeons taught anatomy on unclaimed bodies that came to the hospital to be used for dissection by the teaching surgeons. While training at the hospital to be an apothecary, Smith knew that he wanted to become more. He studied and trained to be both a surgeon and a doctor, as well as an apothecary. He saw surgery as the necessary element of doctoring if lives were to be saved when pills and potions were useless.

Dr. Smith was a registered physician, surgeon, and apothecary with the Royal Engineers sent by the Crown to help develop the new colony of British Columbia. He could doctor, that is check symptoms and prescribe drugs. If needed, he could do surgery and mix and administer medications as an apothecary. Dr. Smith was glad to be doctoring in a time of medical breakthroughs. He was excited about the drug treatments discovered and in use since 1840. Now doctors could administer to patients: morphine, quinine, atropine, digitalin, codeine, and iodine. The stethoscopes common to doctors had recently been improved and were better than they had ever been in Dr. Smith's opinion.

I told Dr. Smith of my desire to become a doctor and asked if I would be able to train to be a doctor here in the colony. He felt it would be some years before a medical school would be established in the colony, but that I could train under him. When I was ready, I could go to London and complete my training by writing exams there. Then I would get registered with the Royal College of Physicians and Surgeons, which would be recognized in Canada as well as Great Britain. Dr. Smith felt that I would be able to doctor in America, as he thought they wouldn't reject my British training, but he could not be positively sure.

Dr. Smith was sure he could get me a small salary as his assistant, but I would have to buy my own medical books. I could use his for study, but if I remained serious about doctoring, I would need my own books and medical journals. It all seemed like a miracle and an excellent opportunity for me. I was ready to bust with my excitement. The doctor said to think it over, and we were both on the steamer with lots of time to discuss it more.

When the doctor left, I knew I had to share my news with the others. I went to Old Man Magee's cabin and knocked on his door, but there was no answer. So, I set off to find Mean Mike, and I found him drunk as a skunk and trying to fist-fight with anyone who would take him on. Not one, but two men were almost ready to close in on him. I ran to Mike and yelled, "There you are, you, ass! No money to pay me what you owe me, but you had enough to buy liquor. You know you go crazy when you're drunk. How many men can you kill and get away with it? The British judge that is here, now they call him the hanging judge."

Mean Mike drunkenly answered, "I don't owe ya any money, Nothing, and Judge Begbie wouldn't hang me."

"Don't be too sure of it," I snapped. "I need you to come with me anyway because Old Man Magee wants you to do a job for him. A fat lot of good you can do for him with you being so stupid drunk," I added.

"Alright, alright, Nothing, quit ya bitching and lead the way," Mean Mike replied, and I led him away from the two men who were ready to fight him, no doubt with the thought of robbery with two against one. Money pouches and wallets have a way of being gone when the loser gets up or wakes up from a fight.

I headed us towards Old Man Magee's cabin, and as we were going, we met Jacque, who was done helping the pilot for the day. He knew a place where we could get some hot coffee, so he took us there. While he got Mike drinking a coffee, I told them I would bring Old Man Magee and Seph there also. I found Seph ready to leave a poker game lighter in money than when he started. When we knocked at Old Man Magee's door, he answered, and he was willing to come with us to have a coffee. We gathered around the table, each with a coffee cup in hand, even Jacque, and it seemed like we all fit together like a well-worn glove. There was an easy talk between everyone. I knew it was the right time to make my announcement. I told the others that I had the opportunity to train to be a doctor under Dr. Smith.

Mean Mike said, "But Nothing, ya will get so involved in playing doctor, ya won't come back to hunt for gold with us in the spring. Who will keep us on the straight and narrow? Ya is my true friend and brother."

Seph spoke up, "Nothing, are you sure you want to listen to sick people who are hard to please? Doing surgery is about as bad as butchering a deer or moose and often kills rather than heals. Doctors deal with death often. Remember our sick baby that we buried at New Westminster? Sometimes you lose a whole family to sickness. We know you will be a good doctor, but it is a tough and often thankless job."

Jacque rose from his place at the table and came and hugged me, and with tears in his eyes said, "Nothing, your heart is genuine and kind. You are so responsible and serious. Maybe you should be a priest or teacher. You read and write and do sums, and we always need teachers. Most of all, we need people like you who can see Indians and breeds like me as one with yourself, a white person."

Old Man Magee spoke last. "It is a great opportunity for you, Nothing, and during the winter you'll see the best and the worse things about being a doctor. A doctor needs to be able to keep a confidence. You knew that I have been sober so I could return to Mae and marry her, no longer a drunk. You never shared that with the others here. It's not just what we say in life, but just as important what we don't say. You know how to keep your mouth shut, which is a rare gift. For the rest of you men, when I get to Fort Langley, I plan to marry a lady named Mae. You are all invited to the wedding, which will be within a few days."

Old Man Magee's wedding announcement resulted in a chorus of cheers and congratulations to him. A steward, an employee of the steamer, asked us to lower our noise as not to disturb others. Mean Mike whispered, "If he only knew we are the Deadly Five, he wouldn't talk to us that way." We parted laughing.

CHAPTER 25
Another Kind of Doctoring

IT WAS THE third day on the steamer, and a young man sought me out.

"Are you Nothing Brown?" he asked me. I nodded yes, and he said that a guy called Mike told him to come and see me.

"What did Mike think I could do for you?" I questioned.

"I have a wound on my arm that is infected, and Mike said you are almost a doctor," he answered.

"Let me see the wound, but I can't promise a cure. I'll see if I can help you with it," I said.

The young man showed me an older deep scrape that was red and swollen with infection. I told him we would begin by bathing it in clean salted water to help draw out the infection. I was able to get a big enough pan that we could submerge the wound on his arm, and just let the scrape soak in the water. The longer the injury was in the water, the more it began to sting, which I told him was a good sign. As we waited for the salted water to cleanse and start the healing process, we talked.

The young man's name was Gus, short for Augustus, and he was broken in spirit. He was returning from the Fraser Canyon with almost nothing to show for his efforts to get rich. The whole excitement of the gold rush had turned for him to bitterness and defeat. He was an American, and his family had cautioned him not to go chasing a rainbow, but he wouldn't listen to them. He would be going home without a pot of gold to face humiliation. He had parents and siblings farming across the border.

I asked Gus if he would feel better about farming with his family when he got home. He said that it would be so much sweeter than being in a mountainous wilderness, always in cold water, searching gravel and mud for gold that was never very plentiful. I suggested maybe his search for gold proved he was a farmer at heart, and that he would be happy farming in his life ahead. His parents and siblings would be worried about him off searching for gold, and they would be glad to have him home safe and sound. He said that the problem was that he was coming back with hardly anything. I said that if he had even a few tiny nuggets of gold to give to each one of his family members, they would be impressed. He liked the idea, and when we had finished soaking his wound, he counted out the gold in his pouch, forgetting I was there to watch him. He looked at me in disappointment.

"I'm short two small nuggets, but it was a great idea."

On the steamer, I had been thinking about my need to give away the gold I had found to help others. I realized that this could be the beginning of my giving of my gold away. I would begin to honor my elders' wishes. I offered Gus two nuggets the same size as his. I told him I was glad to help him have enough nuggets to give each member of his family. I also asked if he had enough money to get him home, and he admitted he was almost broke. I asked him how much money he thought he would need to get home. When he told me a reasonable amount, I gave him the money required. I asked him not to tell anyone of my help to him. It was to be a secret that neither of us would tell anyone ever. Gus's arm was looking slightly better, and he was to see me the next day when we would repeat the application of salted water.

Dr. James Smith came to me and said that he had seen me treating a young man. I gladly told the doctor how I had used salted water on his wound and described the injury to him. I explained I wanted to cleanse the infection and begin the healing process. He agreed that healing comes from the body itself and that salted water was a suitable way to address an older infected wound if the wound can be soaked or covered in the water for a time. He agreed to look at the wound the next day when Gus came back.

Since the doctor had free time, he spoke again of the great hope he held for the advancement in medicine that he was sure was coming in our lifetimes. He was a man that thoroughly liked his own opinions and was given to being able to assess the doctoring faults of the past and able to predict the future of medicine.

The good doctor said that from the ancient Greeks, it had been assumed disease was the result of a disturbance in the body. The body was out of balance because of too much of one of the four bodily humors. The four were yellow bile, black bile, phlegm, and blood. The doctor needed to remove too much of any one of the four through the mouth, nose, rectum, skin, or by bloodletting. Doctors have been prescribing lotions, potions, and pills for centuries to bring relief by putting the body back in balance. Thankfully, the extremes of purging and bloodlettings have been minimized through the centuries. The bedrock of doctoring is letting nature heal or take its course.

The fact that the young man would come to me for help with an infected wound on his arm angered the doctor. He was frustrated that most ordinary people shunned the authority and competence of a trained doctor because they charged high fees. They would instead treat themselves, use midwives for birthing, go to local healers, and only come to a doctor when they thought that they were dying. Dr.

Smith wanted to know how much I had charged the young man for treating his infected wound. When I told him that I had charged the young man nothing, he said that I better get a different attitude if I hoped to be an actual doctor.

What never failed to turn Dr. Smith from frustration to excitement was his trust in the growing knowledge about the causes of diseases. He eagerly told me how the microscope had allowed a Danish biologist to discover several types of bacteria. Edward Jenner, an English doctor, used this advancement in learning to create a vaccine for smallpox in 1796, which was a miracle breakthrough in saving lives. The future would prove the relationship between sickness and hygiene, the need for sterilization of instruments of surgery, the truth that mosquito bites and fleas on rodents, cause illness. Dr. Smith was adamant that disease did not come from God's punishment on those He disliked, or a poisonous cloud containing germs, nor night air. He was sure learning and advancing scientific knowledge would change doctoring as never before. He was determined that all doctors would need to keep alert in new medical discoveries and retrain in surgical techniques and procedures because more and more was being learned about the human body.

Dr. Smith might have continued to expound his views, but the captain of the steamer came to talk with him, and they left together. As soon as they left, Gus returned to me. I thought that his wound must have been bothering him, but it was his conscience.

"Mr. Nothing Brown, I have to tell you the truth. I lied to you. I had money hidden in my sock and some other gold nuggets in another pouch in my underwear. I did not need your two gold nuggets or your money to get home. I am a liar and a cheat, and I want to give the two nuggets and money back to you. It has been a long time since I have felt ashamed of myself. I am sorry I tried to cheat you," Gus said.

"Thank you, Gus, for being honest with me. I promised you that I would never speak of my giving you the nuggets or money. It is done. They were gifts given to help you. If you do not need them, then give them to your family or someone who needs them. What I have freely given you, I will not take back. Use them or pass them on as they are yours. It is a secret I refuse to talk about now or ever again. I will see you tomorrow to look at your wound," I said. Gus left, shaking his head. He seemed even more troubled than when he came. I was shaking my head, wondering to myself if giving away my gold would be hard to do. Would others want to give it back like Gus?

CHAPTER 26
Two to Become One

THE STEAMER DOCKED at Fort Langley, and we fearsome five went ashore for Old Man Magee's marriage. The ship would be docked for half a day, so we hoped the wedding might be a simple, immediate affair. Mae had left word at Fort Langley that she was at New Westminster operating another saloon. Old Man Magee seemed more than a little relieved, and the four of us were ready to celebrate his wedding with him at New Westminster just as well as at Fort Langley.

One of the men of the Corps of Royal Engineers was at the fort and needed a doctor. Dr. Smith and I went to attend to him. He was bedridden with labored breathing. Dr. Smith asked if I could tell if he had pleurisy, emphysema, bronchitis, or pneumonia. Before I could begin to try to answer, Mean Mike was shouting, "Nothing Brown, we need ya quick!"

Dr. Smith said to me that I had better go. I found Mean Mike, Seph, and Jacque waiting for me in the square of the fort.

"Nothing, ya gotta come quick! A steamer has just docked from New Westminster, and a woman called Mae just got off that steamer walking arm in arm with a man. Old Man Magee went back on the steamer for something and hasn't seen the woman and man, yet. Come see if it is the Mae who Magee is figuring on marrying."

We rushed to the dock area where Old Man Magee was walking up to Mae and her companion. We heard Magee say, "Hello, Mae, you are looking prettier than ever."

Mae did not recognize Old Man Magee and answered, "Thank you, but I don't believe we have met before."

"I believe we have in the past. I was shabbier and mostly drunk," Magee answered.

"Are you sure you are not mixing me up with someone else?" she insisted.

"Mae, I told you I would come back to marry you when I was no longer a penniless drunk," Magee said with a sadness in his voice.

"You can't be Wilfred Magee," Mae said positively. "He went off with some lowlives who killed him for no good reason. I heard he was killed months ago."

"It is not so. I'm Wilfred Magee, sober and ready to marry you," Magee said.

There was a moment of awkward silence. The man beside Mae intensely watched the exchange between the former lovers, and we intensely watched too.

"Oh, my goodness, Wilfred, I cannot marry you. This man is my husband Austin," Mae said, as if marrying Wilfred Magee had never been on her mind.

If Old Man Magee was shocked or disappointed, he didn't show it. "Austin, pleased to meet you," said Magee, extending his hand for a handshake. Austin did not reciprocate.

"Well, I wish you both great happiness in your marriage," Old Man Magee said. Then, poised, and as though they had simply discussed the weather, Old Man Magee gracefully and quickly exited the conversation adding, "Meeting you today has greatly relieved my mind. A good day to you both."

We rushed to Old Man Magee's side to offer our condolences, but instead, he said, "Boys, I think I have just been spared a big mistake."

We went into a huddle of talk around him.

I shook Magee's hand and said, "It is an honor to be your friend. I agree with you that you have been spared a costly error."

Mean Mike spoke up. "'T'is a good sign that ya will be back with us to search for gold next spring. Learn some new songs to sing, and a bunch more fiddle tunes for your violin."

"I know I can get you some work singing and playing your violin in whatever saloon I bartend in, and I will be pleased to have you watch my back when things get out of hand," Seph assured Old Man Magee.

"I have been married a few times. Marriage can be both joyful and miserable. Be joyful for as long as you can when you're not married," Jacque said.

I offered to buy everyone a meal at the fort, and during it we discussed our immediate future at New Westminster. We did not linger at our meal and headed to the steamer to be ready for departure.

Walking back to the steamer, we did not notice when Austin, Mae's husband, appeared near us and pulled out his pistol. He fired point-blank at Old Man Magee and hit Magee dead center in the heart. We were too shocked to move except to catch Old Man Magee as he fell dying on the spot.

We closed in about Magee, and Mean Mike began sobbing. It was contagious, and we all openly wept and hardly heard a second shot. We turned tear-filled eyes to see Mae standing over the crumpled body of Austin, her husband.

We learned later, Mae had told the constable that after the meeting with Wilfred, her only true love, she broke down and cried.

Her crying angered her husband. They had hard words between them, and he accused Mae of loving this Wilfred fellow more than him. She said that she did. Her husband impulsively stormed away in anger, saying he would kill Wilfred. She followed him, determined to stop him, but he got ahead of her. She caught up to Austin as he shot Wilfred down in cold blood. She shot Austin before he tried to shoot her.

The constable, a friend of Mae's, determined that it was a case of self- defense. He decided Mae's husband had gone crazy, killing one man, and Mae had to protect herself. Mae couldn't know who he would kill next. So, she shot him. We knew Judge Begbie would never accept such reasoning, but Mae was left alone, and nothing about the two murders would come to trial.

The constable considered us Magee's next of kin, so he allowed us to take Magee's body to bury at New Westminster in the grave-yard where we had buried the baby. At New Westminster, we stuck together, for we needed to get a coffin and prepare and bury Magee's body. Things were getting more settled at New Westminster so that we needed to pay to have a grave site in the graveyard, and we dug the grave ourselves. We laid Old Man Magee in his coffin with his socks on, knowing they could scare off the living and the dead. I was appointed to read from my Bible, and we each said a few words over his grave.

Mae came to Magee's burial and announced she was buying the grave site beside his for her body after her death.

It was a bittersweet interment. Old Man Magee may have been a lot of questionable things in his life, but there was no question he had been a sober, hard-working partner and friend to each of us. The four of us felt connected like brothers, and we knew that if we could, we would help each other always. We filled in the grave and talked of how we could keep in touch during the winter. I would be assisting Dr. Smith and would live at the infirmary. Seph was to be bartending at the same saloon that he had worked at before, and he could sleep in the back room there. Mean Mike was blacksmithing for the winter and could live there. Jacque was working at Fort Langley during the winter. We decided that whenever Jacque came to New Westminster in dealings with the Hudson's Bay Company that we four would meet. Jacque thought it would be every other week or once a month.

We also had to deal with the gold and money that was left from Old Man Magee's life, after funeral expenses. We voted to give it to Mae, but she refused it. We drew lots, and I ended up getting Old Man Magee's gold and money.

I faced my need to give my gold and money away to help others. I thought of Popcorn Pete and One-Foot-Charlie. If I could find them, surely Popcorn Pete could use the money to train as a doctor, and it seemed to me One-Foot-Charlie could use a gift of cash. I checked the doctor's office at New Westminster, where I had helped the doctor. I was pleased to learn that Popcorn Pete was assisting the doctor and that he was thrilled to be learning from the man. One-Foot-Charlie also worked at the doctor's place. He greeted those who wanted to see the doctor, collected the fee in advance, and boiled towels, sheets, and other articles of laundry from the doctor's office and hung the laundry to dry or ironed it dry.

Popcorn, Charlie, and I had a great visit together, and I asked if they would accept the wealth of Old Man Magee. I suggested that Popcorn Pete might want to go to London and write exams there and get the certification as a doctor and surgeon. I explained how Dr. James Smith of the Royal Engineer Corps had spoken of it to me. Popcorn Pete felt he might have trouble reading medical books, but I suggested we could read them together and encourage and learn from each other during the winter. Popcorn Pete agreed that we could and would. Popcorn said that I could entrust Old Man Magee's money to One-Foot-Charlie, who often found miners and others could not afford the doctor's fees. He could add to whatever money they had to get them in to see the doctor. Some had no money for pills. I told them to let me know when Old Man Magee's money was gone, and I would give them some more myself.

CHAPTER 27

The Fearsome Three

AS FALL GAVE way to winter, Seph served Judge Begbie his drinks when he frequented the saloon. When the judge was in New Westminster, he and Seph were the tallest men in the bar. Seldom did another customer stand taller than six foot five. Sometimes Mean Mike would join them for a drink and a chat, and the judge would join our get-together when Jacque arrived from Fort Langley. On those occasions, the judge always joked that his presence made us the Deadly Five again or at least the fearsome five. We told the judge that he could take Old Man Magee's place in our gold-hunting ventures, if he showed up at Fort Hope in the spring.

Popcorn Pete and One-Foot-Charlie met with me often, and we studied the medical books Dr. Smith loaned me. There was a problem with Popcorn Pete's doctor. He realized that his business had increased sharply. Then he found out One-Foot-Charlie was helping those who could not afford his fees by adding whatever amount of money they were short for the doctor's fee. The doctor angrily threatened to fire One-Foot-Charlie. The doctor did not want to have a reputation for helping those who couldn't afford his fees. The doctor was determined that it would hurt his practice in the long run. The poor would swamp his office, and it was only a matter of time until One-Foot-Charlie would run out of money to help them. When the doctor learned that One-Foot-Charlie received the money from me, he insisted that Charlie give it back to me, which he did.

I went to Seph and said that I wanted to give him some money, so he could give it away to those he saw as penniless in the saloon. He said he would think about it, but it did not seem like a wise idea to him. I also went to the blacksmith shop and talked to Mean Mike to see if he would take some money from me and use it to help pay for work done when customers did not have enough funds to pay. Mean Mike did not like the idea, and his boss said that people shouldn't get work done if they didn't have the money to pay for it.

Seph, Mean Mike, and his boss all believed I was foolish. They all agreed that no one ever gives money away just because people seem to need it. One should only give money to help the needy if one can be sure the people are impoverished. The three of them questioned how anyone could prove they were needy. People tend to lie if they think they can get something for nothing. Seph said that in the large cities like New York or London, they have homes for the destitute, and orphanages for children. There you can give your money and know it will be used to help the needy. Here in the gold rush, everyone that is a miner is primarily homeless. Who can tell who has his gold or money hidden and who is penniless?

It became more and more apparent that giving my money away to others in need would not be a simple thing for me to do. I wondered if my elders had ever given money away to the needy as they had instructed me. I decided I would talk about it with Judge Begbie since there must be some appropriate way of accomplishing it. I asked Seph if he could set a time that I could talk with the judge when he was in town again. A week later, I met Judge Begbie at the saloon. He drank whiskey and I water. I explained that I was in the gold rush so that whatever gold I got I would give it to the needy. The judge asked if giving away my wealth had to do with my religion. I explained that I was a Quaker and that my elders had suggested it as a way of me gaining maturity in my faith.

The judge was a student of scripture and quoted the words of Jesus. He said, "No one can serve two masters. Either he will hate the one and love the other, or he will be devoted to the one and despise the other. You cannot serve both God and money." Then he asked, "Do you believe this is why your elders want you to give your gold away?"

"Partly so, because anyone can become devoted to finding, making, accumulating, and holding on to wealth. It is an empty treasure. Wealth easily becomes the devotion of a person's heart. Money has no real permanence. It can so easily be lost or stolen. Our wealth is God's on loan for us to use, our daily bread to be shared with others. Wealth does no one any good in the grave," I answered.

"Do you ever think of keeping the money from your gold searching for yourself?" the judge questioned me.

"Yes, I have thought of keeping it to use for studying to be a doctor," I answered. "I see it this way, that my becoming a doctor is a self-centered desire. How much money will I need for my studies is uncertain. Right now, I have more money than I need to live on, so I'm trying to give money away to help others. How can I do it, in your opinion?"

Once again, the judge quoted Jesus by saying, "But when you give to the needy, do not let your left hand know what your right hand is doing so that your giving may be in secret. Then your Father, who sees what is done in secret, will reward you." Then the judge remarked that giving is one of the hardest things we can try to do. He suggested that if I see someone with a need for money, that I give it to them anonymously. When they do not know who gave the money to them, they cannot return it to the giver. They will not feel a need to treat you in thankfulness or honor. You can know God will reward your act of kindness.

Judge Begbie could see I was surprised and impressed with his knowledge of Jesus's teachings. He said to me that outwardly religious people, like me, forget that they have no monopoly on God or the Bible. He also commended me to keep searching spiritually and to keep helping the needy, not only with money but with respect and honor, especially when they seemed decidedly sinful in their ways. He ended by saying that a judge must give verdicts reflecting the law. Christians need to provide verdicts reflecting forgiveness and kindness as Jesus did.

"Nothing," he said, "When you see me drinking, which I do often, remember that it isn't just the liquor that goes in my mouth but also the words that come out of my mouth and the deeds that I do."

We might have spoken more, but Mean Mike arrived and joined us and so I was seated like a flea between two giant bumblebees. The saloon had become loud and rowdy, and one nasty drunk took exception to our table. He saw Seph serve our table with two beers and a glass of water.

He yelled, "The dwarf is drinking water! What the hell kind of drink is that for a saloon? Throw him out! Let him drink water with the fish in the Fraser. This bar is a place for men to drink. No water drinkers in here. It's an insult to us."

I jumped up on the table and yelled just as loud as the drunk, "Seph, bring me a beer, and I'll drink it, so I don't offend these gents."

The drunk yelled back, "No sissy sipping! You need to drink it down without stopping."

"I will, but you need to come over here and stand in front of me so you can see I have drunk it down without stopping," I shouted.

The whole saloon was quiet and watched the drunk stagger over and stand before me on the floor. Seph brought me a glass of beer.

I held it up and said, "Cheers, brother."

Then I put the glass to my lips and drank it for all I was worth. I drank it without stopping. Then I looked directly at the drunk in front of me and vomited up the beer on him. He was too drunk to duck and got a face full, which left him trying to get it out of his eyes.

I shouted, "Gents, that is why I drink water; beer makes me throw up."

There was a burst of laughter and applause for me in the saloon, and I got off the table and sat down as the drunk stumbled out the door. I looked at Judge Begbie, who was surprised and impressed by my words and actions. I said to the judge, "Never assume that people who appear to have no religion have a monopoly on rude and disgusting behavior."

When the judge quit laughing, Mean Mike said to the judge, "Now you see, with fellows like Nothing Brown, why we were the fearsome five."

The judge remarked, "Tonight it wasn't even the fearsome three, but the deadly one with vomit."

CHAPTER 28
Shrinking Numbers

SEPH AND MEAN Mike were the two who were sure they would continue hunting for gold in the spring. However, I began to wonder if those two gold hunters would endure until spring. Through Seph's friendship with Judge Begbie, a position as wine steward on a Royal Navy vessel was offered to Seph. He would sail from the British naval base near Victoria on December 10 to Hawaii and then return from there by March 8. We were all excited about his opportunity to travel, but also wondered if he might stay in Hawaii, as it's reported to be such a beautiful place. Our other thought was that ships were often delayed and wrecked by storms. Many who went to sea never returned for various reasons.

Mean Mike was enjoying his blacksmithing as never before, part of it due to the attention he was able to share with three young ladies. Mable was a rough and hardy barmaid who had an affection for big miners who had found some gold. Martha was the daughter of the blacksmith for whom Mike worked. The other lady was Ling-Mae, a young Chinese woman who worked at her family's laundry. Mean Mike was sure that he was madly in love with whatever girl that he was with at the time. I cautioned him that he might find in his juggling of his three ladies that he could end up in the loss of all three. He just rolled his eyes at me and said, "Nothing, when you have even one girlfriend, then I'll listen to you."

I was finding being the assistant to Dr. Smith both a blessing and a curse. He was the sort of man that never stopped talking even when he was by himself. He expected me to listen in rapt attention, and to observe him doctor patients and to clean up after and before him. He saw me as his servant as much as his assistant. He had been warned that if you teach an assistant too much, they will begin to equal you, and then they will go off and start their own practice. One thing I appreciated was his willingness to share his medical books. I felt I was learning by my observation of him, and from the study of his medical books.

Things began to get complicated for Mean Mike when Henry Sigurd Arden, a British gentleman and adventurer became a regular in Mable's bar. Mable was sure he had more than enough wealth for her future. Henry was from an old landed-English family complete with a castle at Park Hill named Bromwich or Bromwick or some such thing. He boasted of a pedigree that went back to Anglo-Saxon times. He thrilled Mable with stories of long-dead relatives and especially of one named Robert, who had been executed for supporting Richard Duke of York. Mean Mike was sure Mable and himself had never heard of the Duke of York, and it made no difference to either of them that Henry's relative Robert was executed.

The longer Henry Sigurd Arden remained in New Westminster, and as a patron of Mable's bar, the more, Mean Mike resented him. Mable, however, could not stop talking of Henry and how a second cousin of one of his relatives was the mother of Shakespeare. Mean Mike said to Mable, "You don't even read or write, so why are you carrying on about one of Henry's relatives related to Shakespeare's mother?"

"Well, at least I know a gentleman when I see one, not like a mean-mouthed jackass like you!" Mable told Mean Mike.

Henry had arrived at the bar in time to hear the exchange between the two. Henry demanded that Mean Mike should apologize to Mable. Mean Mike refused. Henry recovered a glove from his belt and slapped Mike across the face with the glove. Henry then said to Mean Mike, "I challenge you to a duel with pistols at dawn."

Mean Mike said, "No way, we will finish this right now with our fists. Put up your fists and fight right here."

"Certainly," Henry said and hit Mean Mike in the jaw, which sent Mike's head backward. Two more finely placed punches by Henry and Mean Mike knew the Englishman was a well-trained boxer. Mean Mike knew he needed a diversion, so he screamed at the top of his voice, "Stop," and Henry paused slightly. That was what Mean Mike needed, and he hit Henry with a right that staggered Henry and crumpled him to the floor.

Mable rushed to Henry, calling Mike a stupid brute that she never wanted to see again. Right there, Mike went from three girls to two in about ten minutes. Leaving Mable and Henry at the bar, Mike walked off in a bit of a daze.

He passed the laundry and went in to say hello to Ling-Mae. Mike told Ling-Mae about his fight, and Ling-Mae came close to check his face where he had been punched. When she came close to Mean Mike, he kissed her. She liked the kiss and kissed him back. The problem was that her father came from the back of the laundry and started yelling. When Mean Mike was slow to end the kissing, the father picked up a large sword and continued yelling in Chinese and advancing towards Mike with the sword. Mean Mike made a hasty retreat. Then there was one girl left for Mike.

Martha and her father heard the gossip of Mike's bar fight and the father of a Chinese girl chasing Mike partway down a street with a sword. Martha left to visit relatives in Victoria.

Mean Mike was fired from his job at the blacksmith shop. He spent half a week drinking in sorrow at the loss of his three girlfriends. He was rescued when Jacque arrived at New Westminster looking for a blacksmith for Fort Langley. The blacksmith there was kicked in the stomach by a horse he was shoeing, which resulted in his death. Mean Mike was willing to spend the rest of the winter at Fort Langley.

Jacque had other news, which was that he was being sent to the Hudson's Bay fort at Yale. They needed staff there as it was much busier there than at Fort Langley. Jacque would not likely get back to New Westminster during the winter. He would meet those ready to search for gold in the spring at Fort Hope. Mean Mike said that he would come to visit me in the winter whenever he could, as Fort Langley was not so far away. I said I would visit him at Fort Langley if I got a chance. It was hard to see Jacque leave for Fort Yale because it was back in the thick of the gold rush. He assured us he had friends at the Hudson's Bay Company there and would see us in the spring if he decided to go gold hunting again. Mean Mike said that he would come to Fort Yale and get him if Jacque did not show up on April 11.

Although I had Popcorn Pete and One-Foot-Charlie to study with, I felt like an orphan with Seph and Mean Mike gone from New Westminster and Jacque no longer coming to visit. Four weeks after Mike left for Fort Langley, Dr. Smith shut the infirmary to his patients and went to Victoria. The doctor would be gone for about two weeks on personal business. I decided to go to Fort Langley and see Mean Mike. It was not hard to take a steamer between New Westminster and Fort Langley.

It was a sunny but cold morning when I arrived in the second week of December. I was looking forward to seeing Mean Mike, but he was not at Fort Langley. He had left word at the fort for me that he had gone to an Indian village to marry himself a wife. Mean Mike was sure that he would be at Fort Hope on April 11, and he would see me then.

Popcorn Pete and Charlie were amazed to see me back so soon. We three questioned if any Indian village would stand for long as Mean Mike had a way of knocking everything over. We also thought that Mike would never stop at one wife but have several. The truth was that I missed Mean Mike, Seph, and Jacque. I felt like I was missing an arm and part of my soul. The three men gave me confidence in myself when we were together. I realized that we might not meet again. Would I leave Dr. Smith in the spring to go searching for gold once more? April 11 would challenge every one of us to begin again as partners. Not every single one of us would take up the challenge, or would we each do so?

CHAPTER 29
Two Weeks

I WAS DETERMINED to make the best of the two weeks when Dr. Smith was in Victoria. I dedicated the time to give my money away to the needy. I did it secretly. I went first to the saloon that Seph had worked in before he left for Hawaii. I knew the owner there and asked if I could talk to him about becoming a partner in his business. I told him I was going to show him how to increase his business, and all he had to do was let me provide some extras for his bar customers.

I explained, in the beginning, there would be no expense to him. If I increased the number of people in his bar and his profits after a week, we would discuss the terms for me becoming a partner with him. The way I would begin to increase his business was straight-forward. I would provide hard-boiled eggs daily for the next week. Customers could eat one or two per visit to the bar for free. There would also be a big pot of soup that people could get one cup for free during the day. At night men could nibble on crackers and drink a hot cup of tea or coffee for no charge.

The boss of the saloon was very doubtful that my plan would increase his profits. He was motivated by the fact that it would not cost him anything. He was skeptical and thought I had no business sense. In his mind, he had decided that he would never have me as his business partner. Yet, he permitted me to try the extras at his bar for a week.

The cost for the eggs was high, as well as for the soup, the tea and coffee, and crackers. They added up to a sizeable sum and cut into the money from Old Man Magee. I felt that he would want it shared with those who frequented saloons as he had. He knew that often, those in bars were hungry and nearly penniless. His money gave a bit of food and a hot drink for many with little and nowhere to go.

For one week, I spent my time frantically focused on making sure there were boiled eggs, soup, crackers, tea, and coffee at the saloon. I was so busy preparing and filling up the free extras that I could not tell if the bar was busier, or if the extra people increased the owner's profits. I was in and out of the saloon and seen as an employee and a religious nut.

The fact that I did not swear often, or curse freely was considered suspicious. I was recognized as the character who didn't drink beer because it made me vomit. I made lots of regular customers uncomfortable because I was quiet, respectful, and considerate of others. Many want a saloon to be loud, rowdy, raw, and an uninhibited place. Even those that resented me began to ignore me and accept me. I became a helper to some miners who wanted help reading or writing letters. Sometimes, I was amazed that the meanest drunk could ask for forgiveness and a blessing when sober. I was, after a week, the little guy who was almost a doctor and nearly a priest or preacher.

In one week, the saloon had developed great fame. A place you could get something free was worth checking out. The bar was overflowing daily, and the profits had significantly increased. The owner was both shocked and propelled into greed. He told me that my scheme to grow his business had not worked and that whatever I had spent on boiled eggs, soup, crackers, tea, and coffee was my problem. We both knew he was dishonest about the success of his business in the week. He had no intention ever of having a partner. He suggested I try to become a partner with someone else. I had used up nearly one-third of Old Man Magee's money.

Two days after my dismissal, the owner of the saloon had a change of heart. The owner requested a business meeting with me. He admitted that he had acted rashly. The first day of my absence, my free food and drink were all missed by the customers. When they asked when I and the free provisions would be back, they rejected the answer that they would not be back. A number of customers said that they would not be back either. Word spread fast, and the saloon was ignored. Business went from bustling to bust in one single day.

I leveled with the owner of the saloon that providing the extras at his bar was a way to help miners secretly. I had been able to do it briefly for that week, but shortly Dr. Smith would be back, and I would be busy being his assistant. I shared the truth that I had some, but not an unlimited amount of money that I wanted to give to those in need. I said if he would split the food cost with me, he could keep providing free extras at his saloon much longer before my money was used up. It would mean some of his staff would need to boil eggs, make soup, and make tea and coffee. I also asked if I could have a small table at the back of his saloon three nights a week and on Sunday evening. There I would help those that wanted help as an almost doctor and almost preacher. The owner was open to everything I said to him.

I had three days before Dr. Smith was to be back, so I got busy supplying the saloon with boiled eggs, soup, crackers, tea, and coffee. By the end of the third day, other workers at the saloon were ready to take charge of preparing and serving these items. Every week, according to my word, I would meet with the owner and give him half of the cost for the food.

At a small table at the back of the saloon I helped people who wanted it. I did not expect many miners to come to see me, but I was wrong. I had thought it would be questions about health issues of pains, strains, cuts, infections, etc., but I had as many who wanted to speak to me about God's word to deal with sin, guilt, anger, fear, depression, and more. It was clear people always need healing for their bodies and their souls. Sadly, too often, their souls and their relationship to God and others are neglected.

It would seem hope would be limitless among the men searching for gold in the wilderness. Spitting in the face of danger to be rewarded with gold beyond measure can be a powerful dream until it becomes an empty reality. A few men will never take no for an answer. A small few will endure every hardship and failure and never give up their dream of riches. Many of the miners lived with doubt and discouragement. I was a person that could be a safe ear to confess frustration and uncertainty. Many men refuse to admit what might be considered a weakness.

Drunk men unload to other drunk men because none of them tend to remember who said what the next day. Drunk men can take offense at what is said between them and fight with each other or kill each other. They may fight often but only kill each other occasionally. I was an almost person, too short to be a real man, not a real doctor or priest, just a weird little guy who you could say anything to because he did not count. I had one rule that anyone who wanted my doctoring, or my listening ear, needed to be almost sober. I would not help seriously drunk people. Serious drinkers and drunks tended to avoid me unless they sought out information from me to help win an argument or to aggravate me.

One man that sought me out at my table at the saloon was Henry Sigurd Arden. I had heard some prejudicial things about Henry as an English gentleman and adventurer from Mean Mike. I tried not to let them color my opinion of the man. He was a forthright young man.

"Mr. Nothing Brown, I am Henry Arden, and I wish to make your acquaintance if you would kindly honor me with your time for a few words," Henry Arden said to me at my back table at the saloon.

"Certainly, Henry. If you need medical or spiritual advice, let me be clear that I'm neither a fully trained doctor nor a preacher. Mostly, I'm considered a person who can help with some medical problems and who will listen to personal problems. If desired, I will comment on personal troubles according to the teachings of Jesus. I can read and write and will help read and write letters for others who want that help. Last of all, I will pray for anyone who asks me to pray for them," I told Henry Arden.

"Mr. Brown, I understand you are a friend and partner with a man named Mean Mike. You see Mean Mike and I were both inter-ested in a certain lady named Mable. Your friend has a powerful right punch that caused me temporary incapacitation. Since that incident, I have found that I may have misjudged the honest intentions of the lady Mable. She turned to cold tea when she found out that my deep historical family roots do not mean that I'm a man of great wealth. I want the opportunity to talk with your friend Mean Mike as I have not forgotten his powerful punch. I intend to see if I can turn a once-powerful rival into an ally," Henry Arden said.

"Mr. Arden, I'm a friend of Mean Mike, but presently he is not here. I do not expect to see him until spring. If I do have contact with him, I will inform him of your desire to connect with him in a friendly manner. It is my opinion he will be open to that, but I caution you to make sure he is sober because his drinking can bring a mean streak out in him," I informed Henry Arden.

"Mr. Nothing Brown, thank you for your information, but could I ask if you lead religious services on Sunday evenings? I was raised in a high Church of England parish and prefer the simpler, lower chapel type of service. I should like to hear you preaching God's word as I miss church services," Henry Arden said.

"Could I call you Henry, or would you be offended?" I asked him.

"Yes, certainly, but I hesitate to call you Nothing. Is that your given name?" Henry asked me.

"It is a nickname, but it seems to fit me, and I've grown comfortable with it," I answered. "I do not preach, but I do read from the gospel of Mark and discuss the passage if those present are open to it. Would you consider joining in the discussion with me?" I asked Henry.

"I will come out and join the people assembled for God's word. I imagine that it might be a small number. Perhaps like a few sheep among a pack of wolves," he commented.

"Every person, no matter how sinful or how godless they may seem to be, has the light of God in them. Openly religious people do not always let God's light of forgiveness, peace, and mercy shine in their lives. We are all in a struggle to love God by loving each other. God works in the sheep but also in the wolves. Sometimes I may be more of a wolf than a sheep. I have a terrible temper that won't stay tamed," I said.

Henry and I might have talked longer, but a young man came to the table with a cut bleeding badly, and I needed to stop the bleeding and close the wound with some stitches. Henry offered to help hold pressure on the cut once I had a clean cloth on the injury. Once we got the bleeding stopped, I stitched the wound, closing it with six stitches. The young man was shaken badly at the sight of his own blood, and Henry said that he would walk with the young man to his tent to see that he was okay. I was thankful for his help.

CHAPTER 30
Trying to Build Christmas Joy

ONE MIGHT SAY that in a gold rush, it is always the season to be greedy. The desire to find gold is in the air and on the hearts and minds of men searching for it. People are there to strike gold, get rich, and go home. The winter weather at New Westminster was not extremely harsh or bitter. At Fort Hope, Fort Yale, the river, and mountains beyond the forts, the winter was powerful and unforgiving to those not prepared for the reality of freezing to death. Searching for gold at Fort Hope and Fort Yale was limited by the winter weather. We had headed for New Westminster because it was on the coast and warmer than inland. Winter slowed the searching for gold, and that intensified frustration and boredom.

As December neared the twenty-fifth day, everywhere in the colony of British Columbia, gold seekers waited and longed for spring and the ability to search for gold without restriction once more. At the saloon, I found that the approach of Christmas Day resulted in more miners telling me of homesickness. I talked with the saloon owner, who was open to me putting up a Christmas tree. I thought a concert for Christmas Eve might stir up a desire for the joy of Christmas. Drunkenness, fights, thieving, killings, and suicides threatened to scare Santa and the Christ Child away from New Westminster that December.

Instead of being at the saloon at my table three nights a week and Sunday evening, I was there only two nights a week plus the Sunday evening. The first week was both so busy and so troublesome that the owner said that I could have no more than two nights a week at my table. The patrons of the bar were okay if I was there, and nobody came to see me. The first night it was hard to concentrate on their drinking, gambling, and making time with bar ladies, because of a line of men waiting to ask me for help with their many doctoring problems.

The first fellow had a rash that covered his arms, chest, and back. He shed his shirt so I could see it clearly. The regular drinkers couldn't ignore a shirtless man covered in an ugly red rash. The second man had stepped on something that punctured his shoe and penetrated his foot. He came hobbling into line with his injured foot lifted off the floor, leaning on a friend. His injured foot was shoeless in a bloody sock dripping blood. These two men were enough to upset a very drunk fellow who pulled his gun and fired it into the ceiling of the saloon. His shots resulted in a silence which he proceeded to fill with profanity and his opinion.

"I came here to drink and enjoy myself. I don't want to see nobody's damn rash or a foot dripping blood. This bar is no place for the wounded and diseased. This here place is a saloon. Kick that dwarf, Nothing, out of here and send his collection of sickos with him," the drunk yelled. There was clapping and shouting in support of the drunk's point of view.

The man I had talked to about his rash went straight for the drunk and said, "I'm not diseased, you drunken ass." He then pushed the drunk.

The drunk yelled at the man, "Get the hell away from me. You'll give me your damn rash."

"I sure as hell will," the man said, taking off his shirt. "I'm going to make you lick every inch of my rash." The man threateningly lunged for the drunk who began screaming and running around the saloon to get away from the man and his rash. Everyone made room for the man with his bad rash. It was apparent that no one wanted to be in contact with that rash.

The owner of the saloon stepped in front of the man with the rash and yelled, "Stop right there! I'm the owner of this bar. Put your shirt on and go on home." Then he asked, "Has Nothing told you how to treat your rash?"

"He has told me what to try. I'll leave now," the man said, and left.

The owner then yelled, "You men who want to see Nothing, wait outside and come in one at a time to see him. Don't line up in here a dozen deep, just one at a time. I don't want you upsetting my customers." That received a cheer of approval from the drinkers, and those wishing to see me waited outside the saloon and came in to see me one at a time.

Most of the men speaking to me at the bar two nights a week reflected a desire to find cures for head and toothaches, sprains, broken bones, bruises, cuts, burns, skin rashes, sores on their feet, bleeding from broken noses from fights, stab wounds, gunshot wounds, severe long-term vomiting or diarrhea, flu, colds, fevers, coughs, and the like.

I tried to see those wanting medical advice or help for their body first because often, it tended to take a shorter time to deal with them. The needs of the soul tended to involve more listening and talking because depression and mental instability are often more complicated than a cut or sprain.

Sunday evenings, I tried to keep a focus on the encouragement of us all around God's word and prayer. We met in the early evening before the saloon became full and loud. Some Sunday evenings were brief meetings. Some were longer, depending on the enthusiasm of the individuals for discussion and personal sharing. Henry Arden was a regular, and Judge Begbie occasionally came according to his travels about the colony. If someone wanted to talk about their sin, guilt, hate, revenge, jealousy, lust, anger, and other personal concerns, I would listen to him and offer the example and words of Jesus. If people wanted the whole group to hear their struggle with anger or hate or some other topic, we would have a group discussion but with a focus on how God's word applied. Our attendance went up and down and reflected the flow of people passing through New Westminster and the saloon.

Henry Arden asked the owner if we could hold a service on Christmas Day at the saloon and be allowed to have the singing of carols. Usually, our services were quiet affairs so as not to disturb the owner's customers. For one brief service, we did not want to have hushed words huddled quietly together. Henry paid the owner for us to use his saloon for one half hour on Christmas Day. For thirty minutes, the bar was to be the place of a Christmas concert. We made several signs announcing the event and made sure everyone was invited. The Christmas concert took on a life of its own.

Henry Arden collected volunteers for a choir as he was eager to lead them in the singing of carols. Judge Begbie offered to do a solo of "O Holy Night," which he said was a beautiful new carol of the previous decade, well suited to his operatic voice. Popcorn Pete and One-Foot-Charlie offered to close the concert with "Silent Night." One-Foot-Charlie had been playing Old Man Magee's violin, and Popcorn Pete was set to sing and play the banjo to "Silent Night" in the bluegrass style of Tennessee. Henry insisted I preach a sermon for Christmas Day because just reading the Christmas story from

Luke 2 was not good enough. I felt that we had an awful lot of things going on in the Christmas concert. I did not want the wonder of the birth of Jesus to get lost in our program.

CHAPTER 31
Time Stood Still

THE TIME FOR our saloon Christmas concert burst around me as scheduled. Henry's ten-man choir led off the concert with the carols "O Come, All Ye Faithful" and "Joy to the World," as the bar filled up with miners.

The owner of the saloon addressed the crowd with these words, "Seeing as it is Christmas Day, for this here concert behave yourselves, fellows. The service will be short, afterward drinking and swearing will resume as normal. If you don't want to be part of this concert, leave and come back later."

No one left, and I offered this prayer, "Lord, you know we are here looking for gold. Gold was a gift the Wise Men brought the baby Jesus at the first Christmas. Help us to see You, in and among us, as we pan for gold. Amen."

Oscar, a gigantic bartender, offered to tell the Christmas story. He said, "Listen up! The Bible says that everybody had to be counted so the Roman governor could tax them. So, Joseph took Mary his pregnant wife-to-be to Bethlehem to be counted for taxes. When they got to Bethlehem, it was crowded, and they stayed in a stable. There she gave birth to her firstborn Son. They called the baby, Jesus, and they put the baby in a manger. Judge Begbie will now sing a

165

song called, 'O Holy Night.' He is so tall he can see each of you, and he will know if you are not listening. He ain't called the hanging judge for nothing."

The crowd laughed, and the judge sang his powerful "O Holy Night," hitting the high notes with such perfectness that everyone was spellbound. When he finished, the room was dead silent and then erupted in spontaneous applause.

Oscar continued telling the Christmas story. "There is more to the Christmas story. There were shepherds out in the open country watching their sheep through the night. An angel of the Lord appeared to them. The angel said to them while shining a great light around them, 'I bring you good news and this good news is for all people. A savior has been born this day in Bethlehem. He is Christ the Lord. Go there and see for yourself, for you will find the babe wrapped up in swaddling clothes and lying in a manger.' Then a whole host of angels said, 'Glory to God in the highest, and on earth peace, goodwill toward men.' As soon as the angels were gone, the shepherds took off for Bethlehem and found Mary and Joseph, and the babe lying in a manger and went back to their sheep glorifying and praising God. The choir will sing 'Hark! The Herald Angels Sing.' Sing along if you want to."

I was surprised that many of the men in the saloon joined in the carol. Oscar said, "Now Nothing Brown is going to say a few words about the baby Jesus born at Bethlehem. Nothing, you better stand on the bar or people will be wondering where you are." I climbed on the bar, which was a narrow plank. Someone yelled from the back of the saloon, "Don't give him any beer, or he'll puke on you." There was lots of laughter.

When it died down, I said, "You know I'm just a bit of a doctor and a bit of a preacher, so I'm like the shepherds out in the fields. They knew about sheep but not much about angels or a Savior. Maybe they felt that seeing and hearing angels must mean that they were drunk or out of their minds. They had heard of the old prophecy that God would give to his people a Messiah or Savior, but then again, maybe God had changed His mind. There were lots of doubts that the Savior would ever come to help them. It is like looking for gold. They say that there is gold to be found, but will it happen to you? Will you find enough gold to save you from debt for the rest of your life?

"The people had a right to be doubtful, for the Romans had conquered them, and things were going from bad to worse. Then suddenly, God sent angels to tell the shepherds that the Messiah has been born, and they could go to prove it as the truth, by walking into Bethlehem and finding a babe in a manger there. They went and saw with their own eyes that the baby was there, and they knew God hadn't forgotten his people. They knew God keeps his word. God loves every one of us, and He showed his love in sending his Son, born as a baby in Bethlehem.

"Some would say shepherds are not much, not like a king or royalty, but God loves each of us the same, king or shepherd because He knows we are all sinners needing his love and forgiveness. His forgiveness and love are free for the taking like the gold you pick up from your gold pan. Christmas Day helps us know God loves sinners, and we all need his love, for we are all good at sinning. Amen."

Oscar loudly bellowed, "Did you call me a sinner? Those are fighting words, Nothing Brown!"

I shouted back just as loudly, "Yes, I did, and I mean it! I called us all sinners, and that goes for Judge Begbie as well. God is perfect, and Jesus, His Son, came to be perfect for us all because none of us are perfect. Oscar, you are not perfect and never will be this side of heaven. Trust Jesus because he shares his perfectness with anyone who wants it."

Oscar loudly said, "Maybe I will. When you said Amen, does that mean you are done talking?"

"Almost," I said. "I am going to say the Lord's Prayer, and anyone can say it with me if they want to." I prayed the Lord's Prayer a good number of those present joined in praying. Then Oscar announced that Popcorn Pete and One-Foot-Charlie would sing, "Silent Night" to close the concert. The miners gave loud applause for their performance for the fiddle and banjo were a great hit as well as their singing.

The owner of the saloon announced one free drink to those in the bar for Christmas Day. The drinking, laughing, and swearing returned the bar to its natural state within a couple of minutes. The choir, Judge Begbie, Henry Arden, Popcorn Pete, One-Foot-Charlie, and I lingered as a group at the back of the saloon wishing each other a Merry Christmas. Oscar, the giant bartender, came to our group, and he told us his dad was a pastor in Kansas. We were all happy with our concert, but some others were not.

Someone called my name, and our group went silent. A miner asked, "Nothing, could I have a word with you outside? It won't take long. I would like to say thanks for this concert here today."

I said, "Speak freely right here; these are my friends, and they also helped in the concert."

"Okay, all of you come outside so that we can give you our thanks," the man said.

"Are you willing?" I asked the group. "Sure, we can go out," they answered. We followed the man outside. Outside the saloon, there were fifteen or so men.

The man leading us said, "We want to show our thanks to Nothing Brown first, then we will thank the rest of you. Nothing, come here to get what is coming to you."

"Wait a minute!" Oscar, the bartender, said. "What kind of thanks do you have in mind? You guys don't look very thankful to me."

"He was on our drinking bar telling us that God loves us. We plan to nail him to the wall as a trophy for us who don't give a damn about God. We'll see how many of you in the choir will sing for mercy hanging beside him. Judge Begbie, we don't like you, or your stupid British justice. We will give you no mercy. This Christmas Day will be one we'll remember for years," the leader said. We could see that the leader and his liquored-up bunch were eager to smash our heads together and shed some of our blood.

Oscar challenged the leader, "Were you drunks even in the saloon?"

"Damn right, every one of us was there and ready to ruin your church hogwash, but we decided to beat the shit out you guys out here. That damn bar owner is quick to fire his shotgun. You better start praying, Nothing, because it is time you learned nobody wants you in this saloon or any saloon. You're just about to pay for your sins," the leader bellowed with a built-up passion boiling in the alcohol he had been consuming all day. His bluster was meant to cower me and those with me.

"You don't frighten me, you big windbag. Go home and sleep your liquor off before you get hurt," I said.

"You better call for angels to protect you. You're a worthless little fart in the wind," the leader sneered.

"I don't need angels to face you," I challenged. "The choir and I are used to fighting. You'll be mighty sorry if I call for my choir," I threatened.

The leader snarled, "You better do it quick."

I yelled my crazy mad yell that startled everyone. Then, in the same insane loudness, I cried, "Judge, gouge out their eyes! Henry, cut off any ring fingers. Oscar, don't leave anyone of them with a nut." Then I yelled with the voice of the devil, "Fight to kill. Don't let one get away. The vengeance of the Lord upon them!"

As I ran yelling towards the leader, he pulled his pistol and fired, and I felt the bullet graze my forehead, but I kept running and screaming. I collided with him, and this time his second bullet hit my arm. I twisted in pain and could not see much because blood was running in my one eye from my head wound. That is all I remember. I woke up at the infirmary with stitches in my forehead, and my arm bandaged. My head ached, and my arm hurt so bad tears watered my eyes. Judge Begbie was there, as well as Oscar, Henry, Popcorn Pete, and One-Foot-Charlie. "Did we win?" I managed to ask.

I wanted to know the answer, but I lost consciousness before I heard it. The fight gained fame as the Christmas Day Brawl. It was between a preacher with his choir and a group that didn't want them in their saloon. The preacher was shot, but the group opposing him, took off after being beaten by his choir. One version of the brawl said the preacher died. The other version said he lived a week then died. The official version of the constable said that no one was hurt much, and it was a minor skirmish of no seriousness.

The actual truth was that the judge at six foot five, was a great fighter, and likewise, a giant bartender and an English gentleman. No one denied that the preacher's side had excellent boxers. All the members of the choir proved that they could fight as well as sing. The brawl had been fast and furious once the preacher charged the opposing side. The preacher getting shot surprised both sides. It made his choir truly ready to gouge out eyes, cut off fingers, and more.

Circumstances turned in the preacher's favor because the drunks lost their nerve when their leader shot the preacher twice and said, "Shit, now I done it, boys. Every man for himself."

The drunks hightailed it quickly as a choir member with one foot could be heard yelling over all the fighting, "Gouge out their eyes, cut off their ring fingers, and take at least one nut." It was rumored all winter that the preacher and his choir were both crazy and deadly dangerous. Everyone knew that Judge Begbie had enjoyed fighting in the brawl, but he made it clear that he had witnessed the brawl but had little involvement in it. The fighting capacity of Judge

Begbie gained much respect at New Westminster as the result of the Christmas Day Brawl.

CHAPTER 32

Life on Hold

AFTER THE CHRISTMAS Day concert and my shooting, I was depressed and at odds with myself. What good was sharing the good news of the birth of Christ if I destroyed peace on earth by being the leader of one side of a brawl? Instead of turning the other cheek, I led my choir into battle like a deranged, barbaric, bloodthirsty predator. How could I talk about goodwill towards men with my temper and rash actions? I moped about while my arm healed, seeing myself as a nothing preacher and a nothing doctor. Most of all, I sensed myself as a nothing Quaker, lacking love and peace in dealing with other people. I spent every free minute in prayer and reading the scriptures. It seemed like I needed a miracle to transform me into Christlike thinking and acting.

I was not the only one who questioned my behavior. Dr. Smith had received a request for an official report on my position as his medical assistant. The British Columbia detachment of Royal Engineers was a contingent of Royal Engineers of the British Army commanded by Richard Clement Moody. When news of a gold rush on the Fraser River reached the attention of the colonial office in London, Moody was handpicked to establish British order and to transform the newly established colony of British Columbia into a second England on the Pacific Ocean. Edward Bulwer-Lytton, head of the colonial office, wanted Moody in command as the best representative of British culture as an English gentleman and British officer.

Moody was sworn in as the first lieutenant governor of British Columbia and chief commissioner of lands and works for the colony. He hoped to build a capital city at New Westminster. He selected it as a strategic site for defense from the Americans crossing the border and because of its good port.

The detachment of Royal Engineers had their barracks at New Westminster. The infirmary there was where I worked with Dr. Smith, who was under Chief Surgeon Siddell. It took me several weeks to sort out the officers. There were over 150 regular soldiers called sappers or ditch/road diggers; they were the ones cutting trees and marking out boundaries, roads, and lots for the city. These were the men who got sick and injured and needed doctoring. I recognized the detachment commander Richard Moody, his three captains, and two lieutenants, the chief surgeon, and the commissary officer. I had minimal contact with the officers. A detachment chaplain, however, set his heart on having me banished from any connection with the Royal Engineers in any way.

The chaplain was an ordained reverend of the Church of England. He had no respect for me as an almost preacher who conducted so-called church services in a saloon. He felt that I had no right or authority to speak about God's word. It seemed the chaplain had been good at collecting every negative story about me, but not a single kind word for me. He assumed that I was a devil to be leading others to fight in a brawl, yelling for others to gouge out eyes, cut off fingers, rip off nuts, and fight to kill. The chaplain said that I made a mockery of Christian conduct. I needed to love my enemies. He was determined to ask for my dismissal from being an assistant to

Dr. Smith. I simply told him that he should do what he felt was right before God and myself.

I was summoned to a meeting with the chief surgeon, Dr. Smith, Commander Moody, and the chaplain. I did not realize that Commander Moody had been given a character reference for myself by Judge Begbie. The chaplain accused me of conduct unbecoming of anyone who could be considered part of the Royal Engineers.

Dr. Smith made it clear that I was a civilian who worked with him to obtain training in doctoring. The chief surgeon said that I had been helpful at the infirmary. If there should ever be an attack from the Americans or the natives, the regiment would need men like myself who could treat the minor injuries. In contrast, lifesaving operations and procedures could be attended by others. Both Dr. Smith and the chief surgeon were pleased with my steady work and keenness in learning. They suggested men like me, with a medical aptitude and a desire to doctor the sick, should be encouraged.

The chaplain said that it wasn't my assistance to the doctors that was the problem, but my reputation for taking fits in madness, uttering profanity, for being accused of crimes such as murder, theft, and poisoning people. I was not a certified doctor, but I treated the sick at a saloon. At that same saloon, I held religious services without being an ordained clergyman. I did not preach against adultery, drunkenness, profanity, and greed as an affront to God and a civilized society. I encouraged sin and befriended sinners, so my lack of character was a stain on the reputation of the Royal Engineers. I was a bad influence on the sappers of the regiment. The chaplain requested my immediate dismissal from being an assistant to Dr. Smith and that I have no further interaction with the detachment of Royal Engineers.

I did not try to deny, argue, or defend myself. When Commander Moody asked me to respond to the concerns of the chaplain, I said, "Sir, I have been very fortunate to learn of doctoring and surgery with Doctor Smith and Chief Surgeon Siddell. Doctor Smith's willingness to share his medical books has been a great advantage to my learning. I know there is no end to learning in doctoring. I do treat miners at the saloon who most often are without money for doctors. They know I'm not a fully trained doctor, but I can stitch up cuts, clean and bandage wounds, and discuss what might help with pain or an infection. Mostly I offer hope and assurance that they will be okay and if I know they need a real doctor, I help them see one.

"Yes, on Sundays, we hold a brief service at the saloon. I read from the gospel of Mark, and we discuss together what was said in the biblical account. We pray together, and that is the service at the saloon. Sometimes, I use profanity and fight when pushed, but look at me, sir, my size alone shows no one sees me as a threat. I have a reputation of being a nothing little man, not a real doctor or real preacher."

Dr. Smith spoke up. "Sir, I speak on behalf of my assistant who is spending his time to study doctoring. In April, he will join up with his partners and return to searching for gold, or he will go home then. I believe he will become a fine doctor in time. We could use him with us until April."

Commander Moody spoke to Chief Surgeon Siddell: "Do you concur, doctor?" Dr. Siddell nodded his head, yes. I felt great satisfaction at their endorsement of me.

The commander spoke to the chaplain. "Reverend, your concerns are noted, but this is a frontier society, and you will find it lacking in propriety. Presently the saloons, adultery, prostitution, profanity, and greed are open realities. Nothing Brown has brought the gospel of Mark into a saloon. I hope you will encourage him, not discourage him."

Commander Moody said to me, "You are welcome to remain Doctor Smith's assistant until April, and I encourage you to act like a gentleman with honor at all times."

"Thank you, sir," I replied. The chaplain ignored speaking to me from that time forward until I left in April. He did take every opportunity possible to slander me privately and publicly. I seemed to be everything that he felt was worthy of his complete contempt.

January Reunions

SOMETIMES DAYS AND weeks go by with a steady rhythm that is almost comfortable and predictable. It seemed like the New Year, and the month of January would slide by without significant turbulence. We were particularly busy at the infirmary with sappers down with a severe strain of flu, with four succumbing to death. Other than the flu, the need for surgeries and the doctoring of cuts, wounds, and infirmities was lower than usual. I did assist the chief surgeon on a hand amputation because Dr. Smith was suffering from the flu himself.

A miner had been playing cards and was shot in his hand when reaching to collect his winnings. The sore loser who shot the man got away with the winnings. The winner not only got robbed but suffered from an infection and blood poisoning in his hand and had to have it amputated. It seemed like a bitter deal, but the miner was glad to be alive and unwilling to let the loss of his hand define him. The miner seemed to have the same inner strength and courage as One-Foot-Charlie.

In the middle of January, a bad fire began in a group of tents and spread, catching two wooden buildings near them. They were on the other side of town, and I wasn't aware of what shelters or buildings burned. We received at the infirmary the victims. First to come were seven miners clinging to life with severe burns. Then came five sick and suffering from breathing in the smoke and three more dead upon reaching the infirmary.

It was the first time I questioned if I should continue to train to be a doctor. The seven severely burned men were in absolute agony, and I felt both powerless and physically sick, looking at their burned bodies. Four of the seven died within a day, but three lingered for a few days before the relief of death took them. Being badly, burned, seemed to me to be the worst punishment possible for anyone to endure. I questioned if I was tough enough to face as a doctor the times of horrific pain and suffering people might experience. Could I stand with them and help them in their suffering? I was not confident I could.

It was in such uncertainty that Jacque found me at the infirmary. He was on an assignment from the Kamloops Hudson's Bay fort northeast of Fort Hope. He was searching for serum at Hudson's Bay forts and from the colonial government at New Westminster. It was needed to vaccinate Hudson's Bay employees from the threat of smallpox.

An American gold seeker traveling to Canada from the Columbia River heading for the Thompson River had died of smallpox. He had traded with a small group of natives for food, spending enough time with them to infect them with the smallpox virus. His two traveling partners died near Fort Kamloops, and the fort employees recognized they died of smallpox. They sent word to all native tribes to isolate anyone sick. The Hudson's Bay Company would vaccinate company employees and their families but played a wait and see game of indifference to the possible infection and loss of life in Indians tribes. It angered and frustrated Jacque, but he had no power to change the company's policy.

"When they need fur traders, scouts, hunters, and wilderness guides, they prize us breeds, yet see us as inferior because we are of mixed blood. When sickness comes, the native peoples who supply the company with furs for the company's profits get no protection from the smallpox sickness and death. When April comes, you will find me at Fort Hope, for I plan to search once more for gold. I will be glad to leave my work at the Hudson's Bay Company forts," Jacque stated in sourness.

I wanted to lift his spirit, saying, "Maybe by April 11, those in charge of the company will be asking you to become chief trader of Fort Kamloops or Fort Astoria or Fort Alexandria. With the gold rush pushing northward and endless miners ready to sweep the mountain ranges and pan every river, creek, and stream for gold, they need men like you in charge of their forts."

"If I were in charge, they would still insist I turn a blind eye to helping the Indian tribes if the smallpox sickness strikes them. You know that I'm on a soul quest. The soul of this French fur trader and farmer is searching. I am not sad that I came to Canada, for I believe I have a chance to become at peace here before it loses its wildness and freeness to endless settlers. Gold hunters will come like locusts and strip the gold away, but the mountain ranges will be largely untouched. Even cities of the gold rush, like Yale, will likely disappear for their foundation is gold. Once the gold is found, there is nothing left to keep the city alive. I will try one more time in April to gather more gold, for I plan to buy land in this new colony, that will always be thinly settled among the mountain ranges. A land where I can still hunt and fish in peace in my old age. Will you join us for another search for gold farther along the Fraser and beyond it in April?" Jacque asked me.

"I do not know as I'm torn in half about doctoring. There is a desire to help as a doctor. Helping also means watching people suffer in hideous pain, as in the case of badly, burned victims with little way to help them. Pain, suffering, and death win too often, and doctors are powerless against them far too often. It is hard to live with yourself when the best a doctor can do is treat and wait. I thought that studying and learning would make the difference, but the more I learn, the more I see how little I know. If I do meet you and the others on April 11, it is because I will seek more gold to pay for a medical school in London or Europe. By April, I will be certain if I will become a real doctor," I told Jacque.

"The word throughout the company and the colonial government is that your country is near a civil war. If that happens, will you return home to doctor the wounded soldiers and civilians?" Jacque asked me.

"I could not be a soldier as a Quaker and an advocate for peace, but I could be a doctor to help the victims of war. I would serve them best as a fully trained doctor. A real doctor must be as aware as possible to save lives. I do not want just to treat people and wait to see if it works, I want to save lives, at least as many as possible. I just realized what I want to do, and that is to go gold hunting in April. Then after one more search for gold, luck, or not, I want to become the most educated doctor I possibly can. Thanks, Jacque, for helping me know my own mind," I said.

"You are welcome. I have most of my gold left, which is almost enough to buy land, but some more would seal my plans. Last year, we were a good combination of gold prospectors. Old Man Magee was a cement among us that will not be easily replaced," Jacque stated. "I'm glad you are coming in April to begin at Hope. You and I make half of the now deadly four," he added.

"There is one friend of mine who has asked if he could be part of our group of gold searchers. Henry is his name; he's an adventurous English gentleman wanting to turn his little fortune into much gold. He has a family dating back to the Norman Conquest, who holds an English estate that is rich in history and short on money. Henry is a capable boxer and fighter. He is disciplined and gracious and will rub Mean Mike raw. Henry will hold his own with Mean Mike, and after a week or month, Mike will see Henry as a man you can trust with your life," I informed Jacque.

"I shall look forward to meeting him. What is the word on Popcorn Pete and One-Foot-Charlie?" he asked me.

"They are well, and Popcorn Pete studies medical books with me. He is well-liked and honored by the doctor he works with here. Popcorn has been doctoring most of his life and is way wiser about surgery than me. I help him with his reading ability, which is improving greatly. One-Foot-Charlie has been complaining of pain in his leg stump but keeps going like he has no disability whatsoever. He was smashed with a gun butt in his leg stump at Christmas. Popcorn and I hope that it is just bruising and pain from the hit that is bothering him," I said.

Jacque said, "I remember you knew things about Old Man Magee and never shared them with us. You kept his secrets. If I tell you something, will you promise never to tell anyone?" Jacque asked me.

"That depends, with Old Man Magee, what I saw and what he told me were personal and private. If he had killed someone, stole money, was planning to cheat or stab someone in their sleep, I would not have kept silent about it. You decide if what you want to tell me is private and personal. I will tell you to stop if you start telling me what I cannot hold as a secret concerning you," I said.

"I have a young man who wishes to accompany me on my search for gold in April. His name is Claude, who is my son, raised by his mother and her people near Fort Kamloops. He is one of my three children of my youth scattered about the wilderness served by Hudson's Bay forts. Fur traders do more than trade for furs. Claude is seventeen, the oldest of my children. He is now mostly native rather than French Canadian like me. I call myself French Canadian as my relatives all came from Montreal as fur traders and prized their

French ancestry. Claude has had only limited contact with me, but his mother is a fur pelt sorter, counter, and fur bale maker at the Hudson's Bay fort. She speaks English there and has taught Claude the language of the fur trade forts. Claude is not sure of me as his absentee father, and I have an opportunity to be a father to him. If you and the others do not want him to be with me searching for gold, he and I will search for gold alone. I will introduce him as a friend, not my son. They must either accept or reject us as they see fit. You will be the only one to know he is my son unless he or I tell the others. Can you accept this?" he questioned me.

"I will hold the truth that Claude is your son as your secret. Is he here with you?" I asked.

"Yes, he is waiting for me on the steamer, for we are traveling next to Victoria in our search for smallpox serum. Come with me to the steamer to meet him if you can get away from the infirmary," Jacque said.

Dr. Smith allowed me permission to leave with Jacque. We arrived at the Hudson's Bay steamer that they were booked on for Victoria. Claude was on the deck watching the dock activity. I received permission to board the steamer for a brief time, and Jacque introduced me to his young friend Claude, who he said was interested in joining our gold searching group.

I said to the young man, "I hope you are as talented as your friend Jacque in canoeing, traveling through the wilderness, and hunting. Jacque was one of our old ones in our group hunting gold. You look young and fit, so if Jacque slows us down, you can speed him up. I think he needs a young friend like you with him when we go in April."

"Claude, this man is called Nothing Brown because he says little worth hearing. He, however, is a bit of a doctor and a steady worker in the water and mud. There is so little to him that the wind blows him away some days, but then we keep a rope on him to hold him down," Jacque told his friend and son.

Claude was not sure what to make of our banter, but he sensed our friendship hidden by teasing. He would come to learn of kidding, ribbing, joking, and friendly pestering among white men in their bonds. He seemed to be a shy lad, with a twinkle in his eyes and all the excitement of youth. I said that as far as I was concerned, Claude would be a welcome addition to our group. I left them on the steamer agreeing that we would meet in April at Fort Hope.

CHAPTER 34

Never Drink Alone and Never Drink All Your Liquor

JANUARY WAS QUIET at the saloon for my help as an almost doctor two weeknights, and almost preacher on Sunday evenings. It seemed many of the men who came to our Christmas concert enjoyed it. The Christmas story touched religious roots in them that made them uncomfortable. Rather than causing a revival, it caused them to be more distant from their church roots. They stayed away from services that might tamper with their self-images, which thrived on ignoring God.

One Sunday evening after service, Popcorn Pete, One-Foot-Charlie, and I sat chatting when a tall man with a beard asked if he could join our table. He spoke with a thick French accent and informed us that he hated to drink alone. He assured us that he was not a heavy drinker, usually just one drink. He liked to nurse his drink, preferring good company and talk with others to becoming drunk and offensive to others and himself. He said a little liquor is good for the inside, and a little is also good for the beard and hair. The alcohol makes the hair grow. He always left some liquor in his glass to rub it on his beard and hair.

187

He originated from southern France near the Spanish border and was proud of his Spanish ancestry. He was not going to search for gold, but pack supplies to miners. He was on his way to Yale, for he was determined it would be the ideal base to supply goods to those searching for gold along the Fraser and beyond. He had one pack mule that he valued more than a wife. He was confident in time he would have pack mule teams instead of one mule. He had such an absolute conviction that he could provide supplies to miners and towns of the gold rush that we were impressed with the man. His love of mules and for their capacity to deliver supplies over mountain trails and passes was convincing.

The man questioned us of our knowledge of Yale and our gold searching along the Fraser. He was an astute businessman inquiring what supplies miners were in most need of, and what food we ate while looking for gold. He was impressed that we had supplied much of our food with hunting and fishing. He had met Judge Begbie just once and was delighted to hear he was a man of fairness and good humor. Before the man left, he told us to look him up at Yale if we went there. Little did he know that we had no love for Yale and would bypass it if possible. We could not make out the name that he said that he went by. It was Cat or Cast something as his accent was hard for us to understand. Upon his leaving, he rose and poured the small amount of whiskey left in his glass into his hand and rubbed it into his beard and hair. He had only drunk the one whiskey in the time he spent with us.

It was an evening of strange individuals bending our ears. After the French man left us, another man joined our table. The saloon was not busy, and this man also wanted to be part of our table to participate in our conversation in progress. He said that his name was George. He was looking for biblical reasons why he could have more than one wife. In the Old Testament, Jacob had more than one wife.

"How many wives do you want?" Popcorn Pete asked George.

"For now, just two, one Chinese and one native," he answered.

"Why do they have to be Chinese and Indian?" One-Foot-Charlie asked George.

"The Chinese women cook, launder clothes for money, and grow vegetables. They often work with their men on the gravel bars with the rockers. I hear Chinese women can be bought from Chinese men," George answered and then added, "I understand that sometimes Indian women are also sold."

"You want to buy two wives, and you want something from the Bible to prove it is okay to purchase your wives?" I asked George.

"Yeah," he said.

"In the Bible, Jacob had lots of trouble with jealousy and strife with two wives. Most fellows find one wife is plenty in a lifetime. Jesus spoke of one wife and one husband for as long as they both shall live. He did not encourage men to have two or more wives," I told George.

"Is it okay to buy one wife?" George persisted.

One-Foot-Charlie said, "It would make your wife someone you bought like buying a female slave."

"Is slavery legal in British colonies like this one?" George asked.

"No," I answered. George was not satisfied with my answer and went to check it out with the bartender. Bartenders were trusted, I observed, as highly aware of laws and everything legal and illegal. George accepted the answer, "no," from the bartender. It made him sour as he returned to our table, which we were leaving.

"I should be able to buy as many wives as I want," he snarled.

"Take it up with the governor if you don't like it," One-Foot-Charlie said, shrugging his shoulders. This answer caused George to push the table into One-Foot-Charlie, who was knocked off balance and smashed into another table with his bruised leg stump. He screamed in pain and was unable to stand on his artificial foot at all.

Popcorn Pete and I were too busy helping One-Foot-Charlie to care that George took off from the saloon. On closer inspection, we could see One-Foot-Charlie's leg stump was severely swollen and needed medical attention. We were able to get him to my infirmary as I was hoping the chief surgeon and Dr. Smith could help treat the leg stump.

At the infirmary, both the doctors gave us their opinion on the leg stump. Dr. Smith suggested and administered a cleaning and dressing of the area attached to the artificial foot. The surgeon wanted to know who had amputated the foot from the leg and was responsible for the stump and artificial foot. Popcorn admitted, he was the one who was responsible. The surgeon wanted to know where he had trained as a surgeon. Popcorn humbly declared that in his part of Tennessee when he amputated the foot from the leg several years ago, he did his doctoring by doing the best he could with what he had. He had implanted two mule bone pegs in the stump of the leg at the time of the amputation. They let the stump heal with its two bone implants. Then he fit the implants into the wooden foot he made. One-Foot-Charlie used crutches with his wooden foot for a time. Then he was able to walk without crutches. He had done so until Christmas when his leg stump was whacked with a rifle butt in our brawl.

The chief surgeon was impressed by the surgery and bone implants done by Popcorn Pete, with Pete being self-taught. He felt that the injury at Christmas had slightly shifted the bone implants, and One-foot-Charlie needed to leave his artificial foot off for a month or more to let his leg stump heal. For two weeks, he needed bed rest, then he could walk with crutches until the surgeon, and the doctor felt he could use his wooden foot once more.

The chief surgeon asked if Popcorn Pete could stay with One-Foot-Charlie for his two week's bed rest, and in his free time, help the surgeon in his surgeries. The two weeks of assisting the chief surgeon made a big difference in Popcorn Pete's life. He was offered a position as an attendant to the chief surgeon who was eager to help Popcorn Pete become an excellent surgeon with the army regiment of Royal Engineers. By the time I left for Hope two months later, One-Foot-Charlie was walking again with his wooden foot and working in the kitchen for the sappers.

CHAPTER 35
A Broken Man

FEBRUARY CAME WITH all the meanness it could deliver. The owner of the saloon received an offer to buy his saloon. He took the offer and planned to be gone at the end of February. On March 1, the new owners would take over. On March 1, the old owner would be off to purchase a saloon at Yale to be closer to the miners and their gold as it was discovered.

The new owners made it clear my two weeknights of doctoring would not continue at their saloon, nor the free hard-boiled eggs, or a free cup of soup. No Sunday evening service would be held in their bar. The new owners were going to specialize in more gambling opportunities and more ladies for prostitution. I was sure that I could continue to assist Dr. Smith in March, and by the end of March, I had to be ready to commit to doctoring or put it on hold for another search for gold.

It was a Valentine's Day joke, I thought. On February 14, I came to the saloon for doctoring those who might seek me out and found a Valentine note on the table for me. It was heart-shaped and said in writing, "I love you. M.M. Your Secret Valentine." The only M.M. I could think of was Mean Mike. It seemed like a trick he would play on me. I had several men that night who wanted help with medical situations, and I was busy doctoring and forgot about the card.

Before I left the saloon, the bartender said that Molly Madelynn, the head lady of the saloon girls, wanted to see me. Molly Madelynn was rumored to be a merciless dictator ruling her bar girls with a dominant hand. I had little personal contact with Molly Madelynn but had heard endless stories about her. The good stories said that her girls were protected from rough customers, and she made sure no customers were robbed. She did her best to keep her girls and their patrons from possible diseases. I could not imagine what she wanted with me.

Molly Madelynn had a small room at the one end of the bar. There she was the manager of those desiring to spend time with one of her girls. She was not a woman to waste her words.

"Thank you, Nothing, for speaking to me. I have admired you from afar here at the saloon. I have seen your dedication and care of the sick and your kindness with the words of Jesus. I have been amazed at your fits of anger and actions that make you an honest person. As you know, the bar is sold, and the girls and I must be gone by March 1. The girls are leaving as they can find places elsewhere, so by the end of March, they will be finished here. I have a favor to ask you as I am dying and may not be dead by March 1. Will you see to my care in my dying?" Molly Madelynn asked me.

I was momentarily speechless in surprise but then gasped out that I would be honored to help her. Molly Madelynn smiled and said, "Thank you, Nothing Brown, the promise of your kind help means everything to me."

I said, "No one should die alone. I will do all that I can to help you through the days ahead. Are you in pain now?"

"All the time, but so far no one knows of it, but you. I have insisted the girls find other places of employment quickly, as I do not want them to see me sick and dying. You are the only one with whom I need to share my fate. In the days ahead, I will do as you instruct me, and I will see you have money for pain medicine and any other expenses. Whatever of my money is left at my death is yours," she said.

"If you have family entitled to your money, I will see they receive it," I told her.

"I have no one who would admit to me being one of their family," she said humbly.

"Fine, then, I will claim you as my sister, and I come with brothers as friends. You have me, and another brother called Popcorn Pete, and a third brother called One-Foot-Charlie. I will bring them around so you can claim as your very own family," I told her. Molly Madelynn broke into sobs!

I said, "May I give you a hug?"

"Yes," she whispered.

I hugged her but not for long, because she quickly said, "That's enough. I don't give or receive hugs. It is a sign of weakness. I refuse to be softhearted and needy even in my dying. You better go now, and I will send word to you in the days ahead as I need more help."

"I'll be ready to help you," I said and left with a sad heart.

Yes, February came with the meanness of change and death. The saloon died to itself, so a new owner and business focus could begin. The saloon girls left quickly for other workplaces, and Molly Madelynn became bedridden quickly. She died within ten days of meeting with me. Popcorn Pete, One-Foot-Charlie, and I were beside her as her brothers when Molly Madelynn died. None of us knew much of her except that she should not die alone with no one to honor her in love.

We buried her in the same graveyard that held Old Man Magee and the infant Chinese baby. A small crowd assembled for Molly Madelynn's graveyard service. Several of the girls that worked under her, saloon employees, and the saloon owner showed her their respects. When it came time to clear out Molly Madelynn's room at the saloon, we found that her money had somehow vanished, but we did not pursue it.

The last night at the saloon was bittersweet for me. Dr. Smith said that he would allow me to have two weeknights at the infirmary starting March 1. It would be for those with limited or no money to pay for doctoring. I tried to make sure the new owners would send those in need my way, but they were mostly indifferent. Sunday night services would be held at the tent of Henry Arden. Endings never seem right to me. I knew that change waits for no one, but I still resented it.

CHAPTER 36
Time to Gather or Scatter

MARCH 8 ARRIVED, and I thought of Seph who was to return on the navy ship that day. He was a gentle giant in our old group, while mean Mike had been a giant like gunpowder ready to explode at will. On March 11, Seph appeared at the infirmary. He was much diminished in weight. I had a stricken feeling looking at him. All I could see was another Molly Madelynn. He assured me that the voyage back from Hawaii had been rough and that he just needed rest. He said he was going to stay in New Westminster and leave with me for gold hunting in April. I was so happy to see him again, and he promised to tell me of Hawaii in the days ahead. He left to check out the saloon where he had worked even though I told him it was then under new ownership. It was the last time I saw him alive.

Three days later, a constable arrived at the infirmary with the personal belongings of Seph. In his belongings, they had found letters addressed to me as his next of kin. Seph had taken a room at the saloon after he saw me. He had entered the room and not come out. After two days, his room was checked, and he was dead in bed. The constable had been summoned, who sent the body to the undertaker and brought me his belongings and the word I needed to contact the undertaker to determine his burial. This contact I did in great sadness and anguish of spirit. Once again, Popcorn Pete and One-Foot-Charlie helped me in another burial. Henry Arden came and said a few words at Seph's burial as I was feeling broken in two. Seph's grave was beside Molly Madelynn's, and I was in a depression that death could be so greedy to those near me.

Henry Arden stepped up to encourage me and keep me working and somewhat normal as March passed day by day towards April. March 24, Mean Mike showed up in New Westminster in all his capacity to thrive on adventure and danger. As we talked of another gold searching trip about to come, the original group of five had shrunk to three. Old Man Magee and Seph were in the graveyard. Me, Mean Mike, and Jacque were left. Five had been the right combination for us, and we had another set of five for the second gold search. They were Mean Mike, me and Henry Arden, Jacque, and his friend Claude. The only one not certain of going on the second gold search was me. Finding gold meant leaving my learning in doctoring and the use of medical books. How would I, Nothing Brown, become something? April 11, 1860 would mold me in my life by the decision I must make then, to keep doctoring or to search for gold.